THE DEVIOUS SERIES

DANGEROUS OBSESSION

DECEITFUL UNION

POISONOUS DESIRE

TWISTED FATES

THE DEVIL'S KILLER

TOXIC HEARTS

SHATTERED STORMS

DARK DECEITS

BOOKS WRITTEN BY BLUE WINTER

A DARK FANTASY AND PARANORMAL NOVEL

DARK BEAUTY

DANGEROUS OBSESSION

THE DEVIOUS SERIES

BY BLUE WINTER

A SELF- PUBLISHED AUTHOR

THE WEB OF DECEITS

TRIGGERS AND WARNINGS

1. Violence:

- Mafia-related violence, including gunfights, assassinations, and physical confrontations.
- References to bloodshed, revenge, and generational feuds.

2. Abuse (Physical, Emotional, and Psychological):

- Depictions of emotional manipulation, controlling behavior, and physical violence.
- Power dynamics and emotional control, particularly in the relationship between Romeo and Mia.

3. Kidnapping and Confinement:

- The theme of being trapped or held against one's will, as seen in forced captivity situations.

4. Death and Loss:

- Family deaths resulting from mafia conflicts.

- Violent deaths and their emotional toll on characters.

5. Mental Health (Depression and Trauma):

- Characters dealing with the trauma of past violence and mafia-related incidents.
- Psychological struggles, anxiety, and emotional instability.

6. Sexual Content and Non-consensual Elements:

- Mentions of dominance, obsession, and coercive relationships in the romantic plot.
- Explicit sexual situations with emotional manipulation and power imbalances.

7. Betrayal and Family Feuds:

- Generational betrayal and the emotional impact on family members.
- Characters struggling with loyalty to family versus personal desires.

PLAYLIST FOR (FORBIDDEN LOVE)

The story is about a mafia fiction filled with forbidden love, betrayal, toxic relationships and emotional struggle.

Birds Of A Feather by Billie Eilish

Wildflower by Billie Eilish

Take All My Love by Reed Wonder ft. Aurora Olivias

Fatal Attraction by Reed Wonder ft. Aurora Olivias

Issues by Daniel Di Angelo

Take Me To Church by Hozier

Devil's Backbone by The Civil Wars

Cassie by Chase Atlantic

Triggered by Chase Atlantic

Love Me by Ex Habit

Wolf and I by Oh Land

Moonlight by Chase Atlantic

After Dark by Mr. Kitty

The Walls by Chase Atlantic

Dangerous by Limi

Here With Me by D4vd

Vibe: *Painful obsessive love with betrayal and survival under mafia violence.*

To listen, here's the link: <u>Dangerous Obsession - playlist by Blue Winter | Spotify</u>

SYNOPSIS

In a world where loyalty is paramount, a forbidden love sparks a deadly war.

Romeo Giuseppe, a ruthless mafia enforcer, is bound by duty and loyalty to his family. But everything changes when he falls for Mia Bianchi, his sister's best friend. Their love, once a source of joy, quickly transforms into a dangerous liability, threatening to upend the fragile peace between their two families.

As their relationship deepens, loyalties are tested, and hidden truths unravel. Romeo finds himself torn between his heart and his duty, navigating the treacherous underworld of mafia politics, where one misstep can be fatal. Meanwhile, Mia's ex-fiancée, Jamie, is determined to destroy their love and claim power for himself.

With both families vying for control and secrets threatening to tear them apart, Romeo and Mia's love becomes a beacon of hope in a world consumed by darkness. But can their love survive the danger that surrounds them?

As the stakes rise, Romeo must confront the reality that the loyalty and duty that once bound him may become the very forces that threaten their happiness. In this gripping tale of love, loyalty, and power, the consequences are deadly, and the question remains: will their love endure or succumb to the chaos of the world they inhabit?

Genre: Dark Romance, Crime, Psychological Thiller

COPYRIGHT PAGE

© 2024 Blue Winter ISBN: 9781304061119

Cover design by: B. Winter Designs

Written and Self-Published by: Blue Winter

Edited by: B. Winter

Proofreader by: B.W. Reads

DEDICATION

To those who dare to love in the darkness, who find solace in the shadows, and who embrace the beauty in the broken. May this story be a testament to the power of love in the darkest of times.

AUTHOR'S BIOGRAPHY

Blue Winter is an enigmatic author who prefers to let her works speak for themselves. With a passion for crafting captivating stories, she has chosen to maintain a private profile, allowing her writing to be the sole focus. Shrouded in mystery, Blue Winter's personal life remains a secret, including her age, birth date, and country of origin.

What is clear, however, is her dedication to creating novels that resonate with readers who appreciate her unique brand of storytelling. With a humble beginning from a family of four, Blue Winter's journey as an author is one of creative expression and connection with her audience.

FOREWORD

In the shadows, where the light dare not tread, lies a world of forbidden passion and unyielding desire. A realm where love knows no bounds, and the heart surrenders to the darkness within. It is here, in this twisted paradise, that we find the true essence of our deepest longings.

Blue Winter's latest masterpiece invites you to surrender to the allure of the unknown, to embrace the beauty in the broken, and to indulge in the intoxicating thrill of the forbidden.

PREFACE

In the depths of our souls, there lies a hunger that cannot be tamed. A craving for the darkness that lurks within, waiting to be unleashed.

This story is for those who dare to confront that darkness, who yearn to surrender to its power, and who find solace in the shadows. It is a tale of love, of obsession, of the unyielding passion that consumes us all.

Join me on this journey into the heart of darkness, where the lines between love and madness blur, and the only truth is the one we create for ourselves.

PROLOGUE

MIA BIANCHI

In the depths of the human soul, a hunger stirs—a craving for the darkness that lingers within. This void echoes with whispers of our deepest desires, a siren's call to surrender to its power. For some, this darkness is a terror to be avoided, a shadow to be kept at bay. But for others, it is a solace, a comfort, a home.

In this twilight realm, love and madness entwine, and the lines between truth and deception blur. Beauty and ugliness coexist, giving both the broken and the bold a place to call their own. This is an invitation to journey into the heart of darkness, where the only constant is the intensity of emotion.

As one ventures into the depths of their shadows, they may emerge transformed, renewed, and reborn. For within the darkness lies the power to heal, to transform, and to love without bounds. This odyssey into the unknown promises a cathartic exploration of the human experience.

CHAPTER ONE

MIA BIANCHI

My life hung by a fragile thread stretched thin by circumstance. The opulent lifestyle we once took for granted had vanished, replaced by a modest home haunted by echoes of better days. Every step through its halls reminded me of what we had lost and how quickly fortune could shift.

My father's job loss shattered our carefully built lives, forcing us to downsize drastically. Dreams I had once cherished—attending university, building a future on my terms—were shelved indefinitely, replaced by a gnawing uncertainty.

But I refused to break. Beneath the crushing weight of reality, I remained determined to carve a new path, one that would lift my family out of despair.

I often drifted back to the golden, sunlit afternoons of my childhood, memories that now felt like distant dreams. We had once lived in a sprawling mansion filled with light and laughter. Polished marble floors reflected dazzling chandeliers, and the scent of freshly cut flowers lingered in the air.

Exotic vacations, gourmet dinners, and a life of privilege were our norm. My father's six-figure salary meant we floated above the burdens of everyday life, disconnected from the struggles most people faced. My parents, always loving and supportive, nurtured every passion I had. Ballet lessons, piano recitals—everything I touched, I mastered. They beamed with pride, certain my future was written in gold.

But no one saw the disaster coming. The economic downturn unraveled our lives like a thread pulled from a tapestry.

Now, my days blurred into a cycle of odd jobs and late-night studying, every moment spent scraping by to keep our heads above water. Tasks I had once taken for granted—scrubbing floors until my knees ached or calculating bills late into the night—had become my reality. Exhaustion clawed at me daily, but I pressed on.

My parents bore their struggles with quiet resilience. Though worry etched lines on their faces, they never complained, never burdened me with their pain. Their strength was my beacon, a constant reminder to keep moving forward.

And then there was Ginevra—Evra, as I affectionately called her. If my parents were my foundation, Evra was the breeze that lifted my spirits. Her laughter was like sunlight breaking through storm clouds, and her friendship a reminder that happiness still existed. Her family, wealthy and influential, treated me like one of their own, a kindness I could never repay.

Through it all, my goals remained clear: to rebuild my future, ease my parents' burdens, and repay their sacrifices. The fire of determination burned in me, even when the path forward felt like walking on shards of glass.

One afternoon, while scrubbing the kitchen floor, the doorbell rang. The sound pierced the silence, and I welcomed the distraction. My heart lifted—Evra. She always had a way of pulling me out of my worries.

We spent hours catching up, her infectious laughter filling the room. As the conversation shifted, her eyes sparkled with excitement.

"There's a gala next weekend," she said, her voice bubbling with enthusiasm. "You have to come with me!"

The thought sparked something inside me—a flicker of excitement I hadn't felt in years. But just as quickly, reality crept back. Could I step into that world again? Did I even belong there anymore?

Sensing my hesitation, Evra placed a reassuring hand on my arm. "Mia, don't worry," she said softly. "You're like family to us. You belong at this gala as much as anyone else."

Her kindness touched me, but unease lingered. While I appreciated her invitation, I couldn't shake the guilt. My parents were working themselves to the bone, and I was barely managing.

Evra, determined as ever, picked up the phone and called her father. "It's all set," she announced minutes later, her triumphant grin lighting up the room. "You deserve this, Mia, and I'm not taking no for an answer."

I laughed despite myself, her enthusiasm contagious. For the first time in a long while, hope stirred inside me. Maybe I did deserve one night to escape.

"Alright, fine," I relented. "But if I embarrass myself, it's on you."

Evra squealed and pulled me into a tight hug. "I'll take that risk!"

As we embraced, a small spark of hope bloomed in my chest. Maybe this gala could be the start of something better.

But even as I smiled, a question lingered in the back of my mind: Could I still belong in that world, or had I been left behind forever?

CHAPTER TWO

MIA BIANCHI

The next morning, I woke with a sense of excitement bubbling inside me, like the anticipation that only comes with Christmas morning. Evra's promise to help me find the perfect dress for the gala had sparked something deep within—a flicker of hope that I hadn't felt in far too long. With a burst of energy, I leaped out of bed, quickly pulling on my clothes before rushing to the kitchen. Today, I wanted everything to be perfect, starting with breakfast for my family.

As the scent of freshly brewed coffee swirled in the air, mingling with the buttery aroma of scrambled eggs, I found solace in the familiar routine. There was a certain comfort in these small, everyday tasks—the crackle of eggs in the pan, the gentle hiss of the coffee maker. Just as I was plating the eggs, the doorbell rang, sending a small thrill of excitement through me. I knew exactly who it was.

I dashed to the door and swung it open, greeted by the sight of Evra standing on the porch, her face alight with pure enthusiasm.

"Today's the day, Mia!" she practically squealed, bouncing on the balls of her feet like a child who could barely contain her joy. "We're going to find you a dress that'll have everyone talking!"

I couldn't help but laugh, swept up in her infectious energy. Her excitement breathed life into me, lifting the weight I had been carrying for so long. In that moment, I felt lighter—almost free.

We embarked on our shopping adventure without hesitation, starting with the essentials. Evra, ever the queen of indulgence, insisted on treating me to the finest lingerie and accessories, determined to make me feel like royalty. Her generosity was overwhelming, a gesture I deeply appreciated, though a voice in the back of my mind whispered warnings about my father's likely disapproval.

"Don't worry about it," Evra said with a casual flick of her wrist when I mentioned my dad. "Daddy will handle it. Everything will be fine, trust me." Her confidence was like a soothing balm, and for once, I let myself believe it.

After what felt like hours of trying on one dress after another, I finally stepped into a gown that caught my breath the moment I looked in the mirror. The fabric, a rich emerald green, shimmered in the soft light of the dressing room, casting a glow that accentuated every curve. When I stepped out to show Evra, her reaction was immediate—her jaw dropped, and her eyes widened in awe.

"This is it, Mia," she whispered, her voice breathless with admiration. "You look stunning."

I turned back to the mirror, barely recognizing the girl reflected there. For the first time in what felt like ages, I saw myself—truly saw myself—as something more than the burden of stress and survival. I felt beautiful, and Evra's unwavering support was the lifeline pulling me back from the edge of self-doubt.

The rest of the day unfolded in a blur of indulgence. We pampered ourselves with hair styling, manicures, and makeup, each step making me feel more like the girl I used to be—the one who belonged at high-society galas, not just scraping by. Yet, despite the mounting excitement, a small voice of worry remained. How would my father react to all of this? His disapproval had been a constant presence lately, a shadow that darkened even the brightest moments.

By the time we returned home, arms laden with takeout and new outfits, I was on edge, carefully observing my dad's face as we served dinner. His expression remained stoic, but I could feel the tension brewing just beneath the surface. I braced myself for the lecture I was sure was coming, my pulse quickening with every passing second.

Just when I thought the dam would break, my mom intervened with a warm, reassuring smile. "Mr. Aurelio has hired someone to take over your household duties for the weekend," she explained, her voice gentle but firm. "You're free to enjoy yourself, Mia."

A rush of relief flooded through me, but it was short-lived. The doorbell rang again, and I opened it to find Mr. and Mrs. Aurelio standing there, their expressions kind but determined. They had come to speak with my parents about the gala, and I could see the storm clouds gathering in my father's eyes as they stepped inside.

As Mr. Aurelio laid out their plan—a team of professionals managing the house and garden so I wouldn't have to worry—my father remained silent, his face set in a hard line.

"We just want Mia to have a good time," Mrs. Aurelio added, her voice full of warmth. "She deserves this, and we'll make sure she's taken care of."

After what felt like an eternity of tense back-and-forth, my father finally relented, though his reluctance was painfully clear. "Fine," he muttered, his tone gruff. "But I'm not entirely comfortable with this whole gala idea."

As soon as the Aurelios left, Evra and I exchanged a secretive smile. We were going to the gala, and nothing was going to stop us now.

Later that evening, my father pulled me aside, his expression softer than I had expected. "Mia," he began, his voice quiet but sincere, "I know I haven't been the most supportive lately, but I want you to know... I'm proud of you. You deserve a night out, and I'll try to be more understanding."

His words washed over me like a warm wave, easing the tension I had been holding onto for so long. I smiled up at him, a flicker of hope lighting inside me. Maybe things were finally starting to fall into place.

But the next morning, a different kind of anxiety settled in. I needed to tell Jamie about the gala, and I wasn't sure how he would react. After finishing a few errands with my mom, I made my way to his house, my stomach twisting with nerves.

When I arrived, Jamie was seated in the living room, his attention absorbed in a video game. I hesitated, unsure of how to begin. "Jamie, can we talk?" I asked softly, my voice tentative.

He paused the game and glanced at me, his expression already tightening. "What's up?"

Taking a deep breath, I explained everything about the gala—how important it was, how much it meant to me. But Jamie's face darkened almost instantly, his mood shifting with alarming speed.

"You're always doing this," he snapped, his voice sharp and rising in intensity. "You put your friends and family before me. What about me, Mia? Don't I matter?"

I swallowed, trying to keep my tone even. "Jamie, that's not fair. I'm not ignoring you. This gala is important to Evra, and I want to go."

But Jamie wasn't hearing any of it. His anger surged like a tidal wave, crashing over me. "You're going to some fancy party without me? You're going to dress up and flirt with other guys? I'm not letting you go!"

A cold fear crept into my chest as his words pierced the air. "Jamie, please," I pleaded, my voice shaking. "You're overreacting. I'm not going to flirt with anyone. I just want to enjoy the night."

"You're lying to me, Mia!" he shouted, his accusations like poison sinking into my skin. "I don't trust you anymore!"

His words stung, and I felt myself shrinking beneath his rage. I tried to calm him down, but it was as if nothing I said could reach him. He stormed out of the room, leaving me frozen in place, shaken and unsure of what to do next.

A few minutes later, Jamie returned, his voice softer but still laced with tension. "I'm sorry," he muttered, though the apology felt hollow. "I just get jealous sometimes. I don't want to lose you."

Relief washed over me, but a lingering unease remained. "You don't have to worry, Jamie," I said, forcing a smile. "I'm not going anywhere."

He nodded, but the doubt still flickered behind his eyes, dark and unsettling.

As I left his house, a tight knot formed in my stomach. His jealousy was suffocating, and I didn't know how much longer I could take it.

Back at home, my mom noticed the tension I was carrying. She sat me down, her warmth and understanding as comforting as ever. "What's wrong, Mia?" she asked gently, her eyes full of concern.

I told her everything about Jamie's outburst, his possessiveness, and how it was making me feel.

"Mia," she said, her voice serious but full of love, "you deserve to be in a relationship where you feel safe and respected."

I nodded, her words sinking deep into my heart. "You're right, Mom. I do."

For the first time in a long while, I felt a sense of empowerment. I was going to the gala, and I wasn't going to let Jamie's insecurities hold me back anymore.

Later that night, as I crawled into bed, my phone buzzed with a message from Jamie: "Hey, I'm sorry again. Can we talk tomorrow?"

I stared at the screen, unsure how to respond. Part of me wanted to forgive him, but another part of me was growing weary of the constant turmoil. In that moment, I realized I had a choice to make—either continue bending to Jamie's will or stand up for myself once and for all.

And deep down, I knew what I had to do.

CHAPTER THREE

MIA BIANCHI

I hesitated, my fingers hovering over the screen, unsure how to respond. Part of me longed to forgive Jamie and move on, but another part was growing weary of his possessiveness and jealousy. Standing there with my phone in hand, I knew I had to make a decision. Should I forgive him and continue the relationship, or was it time to take a stand and prioritize myself?

Taking a deep breath, I typed out a response:
"I need some time to think, Jamie. Your words hurt me, and I'm not sure if I'm ready to talk yet. I deserve respect and trust in a relationship, and I'm not feeling that from you right now."

As soon as I hit send, a wave of relief washed over me. I had taken a stand, asserted my needs. Now, all I could do was wait and see how Jamie would respond.

The next morning, I woke with a mix of anticipation and anxiety swirling in my chest. As I dressed, my phone buzzed with a reply from Jamie:

"Okay, I understand. I'll give you space. But can we please talk soon? I don't want to lose you."

I sighed, conflicted. Part of me wanted to forgive him, to sweep everything under the rug, but another part—still aching from his harsh words—couldn't let go of the anger. I decided to wait before replying. I needed to see if his behavior would truly change.

As I scrubbed the kitchen walls later that morning, my thoughts wandered to Jamie. His jealousy was suffocating, as though he had me in a chokehold, claiming to trust me but never giving me space to breathe. Every decision, no matter how small, felt like an interrogation.

The sharp clatter of Evra's heels against the kitchen floor snapped me out of my thoughts. She leaned casually against the counter, her eyes glinting with curiosity.
"Oh my god, please don't tell me you're thinking about

Jamie again," she said, exasperated. "I've told you a million times—he's not good enough for you."

I stayed silent, unsure how to voice the tangle of emotions inside me. No one knew Jamie like I did. There were moments when he was sweet, tender, and understanding—moments that made me feel like the luckiest person alive. But those moments were fading fast, overshadowed by his need to control.

Evra rolled her eyes, reading me like an open book. "Mia," she said, her tone softening, "you deserve better than this. Someone who makes you feel trapped and small isn't the one for you. You've got to put yourself first."

A spark of determination lit within me, and I nodded. "You're right, Evra. I do need to take care of myself. But..." I hesitated. "I still love him."

Evra sighed but squeezed my hand with a reassuring smile. "Whatever you say, darling. But for now, let's focus on tonight. We have a dress to pick up and a gala to enjoy!"

Her excitement was infectious. I smiled, letting her energy wash over me. "You're right. Let's do it!"

The rest of the day unfolded in a whirlwind of excitement. We tried on dresses, styled each other's hair, and by the time we were done, I felt like a completely different person. My dress, a stunning baby blue, hugged my curves perfectly, and my hair cascaded down my shoulders in soft waves.

At the club later that night, eyes followed us as we stepped inside. Evra, radiant in red, looked every bit the high-society princess she was. We danced, laughed, and let go, the weight of the past few days lifting off my shoulders.

But as the night stretched on, Jamie's presence haunted me. Though he wasn't there, his shadow loomed large. I imagined his anger if he found out I'd gone out without telling him. The thought made my stomach churn, a reminder of how much power I'd let him hold over me.

Needing a break, I leaned toward Evra. "Let's get some air," I said, my voice barely audible over the music.

She nodded, and we slipped outside into the cool night. The crisp breeze touched my skin, and I exhaled deeply, feeling a sense of relief. For the first time in a long while, I'd put myself first, and it felt liberating.

Later that evening, as I lay in bed at Evra's mansion, my mind replayed the night. For the first time in three years, I questioned why I had let Jamie control me for so long.

Despite Evra's reassurances, a flicker of hope lingered. Could Jamie change? Could we fix things? But doubt crept in, whispering the hard truth: Jamie's jealousy wasn't going to disappear.

What if I had left him when it started? Would I have held onto my dignity?

I pushed the thoughts aside, reminding myself I was here to rest, far from the burdens Jamie and I shared. Mr. Aurelio's generosity had made this escape possible, and I wasn't about to waste it.

The next morning, Evra and I were swept up in a flurry of activity. A makeup artist, hairstylist, and personal shopper transformed me. I watched the process in the mirror, the sense of transformation returning but tinged with doubt. Could I belong in this world of opulence?

Evra appeared in the doorway, her voice soft. "Bella, you okay?"

I nodded, forcing a smile. "Just nerves, that's all."

She led me to the suite where my emerald gown awaited. Once dressed, I caught a glimpse of myself in the mirror. For a moment, I felt like a princess, even if the nerves still twisted in my stomach.

The grand ballroom hummed with life as we entered. Conversations and clinking glasses mingled with the sound of the orchestra. Faces blurred together, their expressions unreadable—curiosity, judgment, perhaps even pity.

Evra's steady grip on my arm anchored me as we made our way to her parents. "Darling, you look stunning!" her mother exclaimed, pulling me into a warm embrace.

Small talk flowed easily, but my mind drifted. When had admiration turned into pity?

And then I saw him.

Romeo strode toward us, his gaze piercing through the crowd until it locked onto mine. My breath caught as he reached me, his voice low and intense.
"Mia, you shine," he murmured, sending a shiver down my spine.

Evra squeezed my hand, grounding me, but Romeo's presence left me breathless.

CHAPTER FOUR

ROMEO GIUSEPPE

As I gazed into Mia's eyes, an overwhelming rush of emotions washed over me. "Dio mio," I whispered, the Italian slipping through unbidden. How had this captivating woman, once a shy teenager, blossomed into such stunning beauty? Her emerald green dress hugged her figure perfectly, accentuating every curve as if it had been tailored just for her. The delicate fabric shimmered under the soft lights of the gala, creating an enchanting aura around her.

Yet, even as I admired her, my family's legacy—the Giuseppe Bratva—weighed heavily on my mind. My great-grandfather, Antonio Giuseppe, had built our empire on shrewd deals and alliances in the shadows of power, his hands stained with the ink of countless contracts and the blood of adversaries. My father, Aurelio, had expanded our reach, adding real estate and construction to our portfolio while maintaining the more... creative ventures that fueled our wealth. Our name carried weight, whispered with both fear and respect in the dark corners of the city. Rumors of ties to the infamous Five Families of New York floated around us, unspoken truths buried beneath polite conversation at elegant gatherings like this one.

Tonight's gala was a testament to our influence, a luxurious display of opulence that masked the underlying tensions in the air. Crystal chandeliers hung overhead, casting a warm glow on the polished marble floors, while guests in tailored suits and elegant gowns mingled, their laughter echoing off the walls. Yet, beneath the glittering facade, I sensed an undercurrent of unease. Rivalries with families like the Gambinos and Luccheses simmered just below the surface, their animosities festering like open wounds. New threats—Mexican cartels and Asian triads—waited in the shadows, poised to strike when we least expected it.

Our fortune had been built on a web of secrets—shell companies, proxy operatives, and cooked books. I could almost hear the whispers of the city, warning of the dangers that lurked behind the facade we presented to the world. But I knew the truth behind it all: it was dirty money, a carefully orchestrated facade, and I carried the weight of it every day, like a heavy cloak draped over my shoulders.

"Mia, bella," I murmured, taking her hand, my voice low and husky as I felt her warmth against my skin. "It's been too long. How have you been?" My thoughts swirled with questions, each one tugging at my heart. Who was this woman? What secrets lay behind her captivating smile? And how could I reconcile the duty that bound me to my family with the desire she stirred in me?

As we spoke, I seamlessly switched between Italian and English, a habit born from my upbringing. "Mia, what brings you here tonight? You look stunning, as always." The inner conflict raged on within me—duty versus desire, loyalty versus passion. I kept Mia close as we meandered through the crowd, my hand resting gently on the small of her back, feeling the warmth radiating from her. We exchanged pleasantries, our conversation flowing easily between Italian and English, like a dance that we had perfected over the years.

I couldn't help but notice the way her eyes sparkled when she laughed, or how her hair cascaded down her back like a waterfall of silk, each strand reflecting the light with a life of its own. She was more radiant than I remembered, and I felt a longing deep within me, one that I had buried beneath the weight of family expectations.

As we reached the bar, I ordered drinks, never breaking her gaze, as if the world around us had faded away. "Mia, tell me, what have you been up to all these years?" I asked, my voice low, sincere, each word laced with a curiosity that had been brewing for far too long.

She smiled, though there was something guarded in her expression, a flicker of vulnerability that made my heart ache. "Romeo, I've been keeping busy. Work, family—you know how it is." I nodded, but I could sense there was more. There was always more with Mia. I wanted to peel back the layers and uncover what lay beneath the surface of her well-crafted facade.

"I do. But I want to know more about you, Mia. What drives you?" I leaned in slightly, my voice dropping to a conspiratorial whisper, desperate to break through the walls she had built around herself. Mia's eyes locked onto mine, and for a moment, time seemed to still. I felt like I was drowning in her gaze, losing myself in the depths of emerald green, and I knew I needed to be careful. Just as she was about to respond, my father, Aurelio, appeared beside us, breaking the spell that had momentarily tethered us together.

"Romeo, Mia, I see you two have reconnected," he said warmly, his presence imposing yet somehow reassuring. I nodded, but my mind was racing. What did my father know about Mia? And why did he seem so interested in our reunion?

"Mia, dimmi, cosa ti porta qui stasera?" I asked, my voice low and urgent, unable to shake the feeling that something was amiss. *(Mia, tell me, what brings you here tonight?)* Mia laughed, but I sensed her discomfort, the tension palpable in the air.

"Romeo, I'm surprised you didn't know—your sister invited me." I raised an eyebrow, a flicker of surprise igniting within me. "Evra non me l'ha detto." *(Evra didn't tell me.)* Mia's smile faltered for a moment, and I caught a flicker of unease in her expression. "Maybe she forgot," she said, though her voice lacked conviction, the words hanging in the air like an unsaid truth.

I nodded, but my mind raced with possibilities. What was Mia hiding? And why did I care so much? "Vieni, Mia, let's get out of here for a bit," I suggested, my voice low and inviting, the crowd suddenly feeling too suffocating, the weight of expectations pressing down on me. *(Come, Mia, let's get out of here for a bit.)*

Mia hesitated, her eyes darting around the room as though searching for an escape, a flicker of fear dancing in her gaze. "I don't think that's a good idea, Romeo," she said firmly, her voice steady yet laced with uncertainty. I raised an eyebrow, an edge of determination sharpening my tone. "Perché no, bella? What's wrong?" *(Why not, beautiful? What's wrong?)*

She took a deep breath, and when she spoke, her voice was soft but steady. "I have a boyfriend, Romeo. We've been together for three years."

The admission hit me like a punch to the gut, a pang of disappointment that I refused to let show on my face. "Ah, capisco," I said evenly, though my mind was a whirlwind of questions. *(I understand.)* Who was this boyfriend? And why did Mia seem so hesitant to speak of him?

"Dimmi, Mia," I said, leaning closer, my voice soft but insistent, the air thick with tension. *(Tell me, Mia.)* "What's his name?" For a moment, Mia's eyes locked onto mine, and I saw something there—fear, uncertainty, something deeper that urged me to dig further.

"Jamie," she whispered, her voice barely audible above the chatter around us. I nodded, committing the name to memory, etching it into the depths of my mind. Jamie. I would find out everything I could about him, the weight of my curiosity pressing heavily against my chest.

"Mia, devo sapere di più su Jamie," I said firmly, the resolve hardening my tone. *(Mia, I need to know more about Jamie.)* "What does he do? Where does he work?"

Mia's eyes darted around the room again, as though the walls were closing in on her. "He... um... works in finance," she stammered, her confidence wavering. "He's a financial analyst at a firm downtown." I nodded, though my mind spun with possibilities. "Capisco," I said neutrally, my instincts whispering that there was more to Jamie than she was letting on. *(I understand.)*

"And what's his last name?" I asked, my voice low, almost a whisper, the tension thickening between us. Mia hesitated, her eyes locking onto mine, and I could see the turmoil behind them. Finally, she spoke, her voice trembling with the weight of the revelation. "Evans," she whispered.

I nodded again, committing it to memory, letting the name roll off my tongue as if testing its taste. Jamie Evans. I would find out everything I needed to know about him, the determination growing within me like a wildfire.

"Mia, io devo essere prudente," I asserted firmly, my eyes narrowing as I spoke, the gravity of our situation settling over us like a dark cloud. *(Mia, I have to be careful.)* But even as the words left my lips, there was a flicker of resolve in my gaze, one that betrayed my true intentions. I wasn't one to back down, not when something or someone needed uncovering.

"E io sono determinato a scoprire cosa." My voice softened, but the steel in my tone remained, a quiet promise to myself and her that I would not let this go. *(And I am determined to find out what.)* As I held her gaze, I felt the connection between us pulse like a live wire, a dangerous energy that sparked with every shared breath, igniting an unquenchable desire that threatened to consume me whole.

"Perché non possiamo scoprire di più insieme?" I suggested, my voice dipping into a sultry whisper, the air thick with the promise of secrets yet to be uncovered. *(Why can't we discover more together?)*

Mia hesitated, a flicker of uncertainty crossing her features as she glanced back at the crowd. "I... I don't know, Romeo. It feels complicated."

"Complicated?" I echoed, stepping closer, allowing the tension to build between us like a taut string ready to snap. "Or thrilling?" I challenged, my voice low and enticing, my heart racing at the thought of unraveling this mystery together, her laughter echoing in my ears like a siren's call.

With each heartbeat, I could feel the walls around her defenses weakening, and I knew that this was just the beginning of a tangled web that could ensnare us both—if only we dared to take the plunge.

CHAPTER FIVE

ROMEO GIUSEPPE

I walked into the grand ballroom, my eyes scanning the opulent expanse, searching for a glimpse of Mia. The glittering chandeliers cast a warm glow, reflecting off the polished marble floor, but my focus was solely on the captivating woman who had left an indelible mark on my mind. I couldn't shake the feeling that there was more to her than met the eye.

"Che mistero," I whispered to myself, my Italian heritage betraying my curiosity. *(What a mystery.)* It was the only phrase that seemed fitting for the complexity of emotions swirling within me.

Days passed, and my curiosity only deepened, gnawing at my mind like a persistent itch I couldn't scratch. I found myself scouring the internet, combing through social media platforms, searching for any mention of Jamie Evans, Mia's enigmatic boyfriend. Each click of the mouse felt like a step deeper into a labyrinth of uncertainty.

"Chi è questo Jamie?" I muttered, frustration lacing my voice as my fingers flew across the keyboard, desperately trying to piece together any shred of information. *(Who is this Jamie?)*

As the sun dipped below the horizon, casting a warm orange glow over the city, I gathered my loyal friends and allies at our favorite trattoria, a cozy little spot that felt like a second home. The scent of garlic and fresh herbs wafted through the air, a welcome distraction from my turbulent thoughts.

"Ragazzi, I need your help," I said, my voice low and urgent as I slid a photo of Jamie across the table. Gabriele's eyes narrowed as he scrutinized the image, a mix of curiosity and concern flashing across his face.

"Cosa sta succedendo, Romeo?" *(What's going on, Romeo?)*

"You've been distant since the gala," he added, crossing his arms, his expression turning serious.

I nodded, my gaze drifting as memories of Mia's bright smile and sparkling eyes flooded my mind, a beautiful beacon amid the storm of family obligations and unyielding expectations.

"È Mia," I admitted, my voice barely above a whisper. *(It's Mia.)* "I know she's Evra's best friend from childhood, but there's something about her... something that draws me in. She's not just a pretty face; there's depth to her that I can't quite grasp."

Franco's expression turned thoughtful as he leaned back in his chair, considering my words.

"Pensi che Jamie sia un problema?" *(Do you think Jamie is trouble?)* he asked, probing into my swirling thoughts.

I clenched my jaw, the tension building within me like a pressure cooker about to explode.

"Lo so che lo è." *(I know he is.)* "I can feel it. There's something off about him. It's in the way Mia hesitated when she mentioned him, the flicker of uncertainty in her eyes."

As the night wore on, our discussion shifted to strategy, each of us contributing our unique skills and insights. My determination grew, fueled by a sense of purpose that pulsed through my veins like fire. I could not allow anyone to hurt Mia, not on my watch.

But as I delved deeper into my research, I realized something wasn't adding up. The more I learned, the more I understood that Mia's story about Jamie working in finance was indeed true. My eyes narrowed, confusion swirling in my mind. Why had I doubted her? What did it mean that Jamie was exactly who he claimed to be?

As the days passed, my obsession with uncovering the truth began to fade, replaced by an uncomfortable realization. I had been so caught up in my suspicions that I had ignored the facts staring me in the face.

Then it hit me like a punch to the gut—I had been so focused on my desires that I had overlooked Mia's words.

She had told me the truth, and I had doubted her without cause.

My jaw clenched as I scanned the room, determination flooding my veins. I needed to make things right. I had to apologize to Mia and confront my demons, the shadows that loomed over my heart.

Later that night, I met with Gabriele and Franco again, this time to discuss the affairs of the Bratva family.

"Ragazzi, what's the latest?" I asked, my curiosity resurfacing, eager to shift my focus to something other than the turmoil inside me.

Gabriele looked up, his expression serious.

"Not much, Romeo. Just the usual Bratva family drama," he replied, his voice laced with the weariness of our world.

My eyes locked onto Gabriele's, my mind racing. "Any news on the Pavlov front?" I inquired, the urgency of our situation pressing down on me.

Franco shook his head, the grimace on his face revealing his frustration.

"Niente, Romeo. They're still playing it quietly." *(Nothing, Romeo. They're still playing it quietly.)*

My jaw tightened as my desire for power and control simmered beneath the surface, a cauldron of ambition and anxiety.

"We need to stay vigilant, ragazzi. The Bratva family won't hesitate to strike if they see an opportunity," I cautioned, my voice low but firm, the weight of leadership settling heavily on my shoulders.

As the night wore on, my thoughts returned to Mia, refusing to let go. I couldn't shake the feeling that I had misjudged her, that she was more than just a beautiful face in a sea of glamour.

"Dove sono i miei errori?" I muttered to myself, my Italian heritage revealing my self-doubt. *(Where are my mistakes?)*

I couldn't get Mia out of my mind. Our encounters replayed like a relentless loop, each gesture and word etched into my memory. Something about her felt off, yet my instincts screamed she was genuine, the kind of truth I longed for in a world rife with deception.

"Dai, Romeo, focus!" Gabriele's voice cut through my reverie, grounding me back in the present.

I nodded, meeting Luca's inquisitive gaze, hoping to shake off the fog of my thoughts.

"Scusa, ragazzi. My mind's elsewhere," I replied, forcing a smile.

Franco's raised eyebrow spoke volumes. "Mia, perhaps?" he suggested, the teasing lilt to his voice thinly veiling his concern.

My expression turned stoic, but my eyes betrayed me. A flicker of curiosity revealed the truth; they knew me all too well. The room fell silent, the hum of the espresso machine the only sound. My friends knew better than to push me further, yet the weight of their expectations hung in the air like an unspoken challenge.

As the night wore on, Mia dominated my thoughts. Our connection was undeniable, yet my loyalty to my family and my demons made me hesitant. The darkness within me threatened to consume her innocence, and I was torn between desire and duty.

"Maybe," I admitted, the word barely above a whisper, a fragile admission of my growing feelings.

The admission hung in the air, a challenge to myself. Could I risk exposing Mia to my world's cruelty? Or would I protect her, keeping her safe from the shadows that haunted me? My heart raced with uncertainty, a tempest brewing inside me as I contemplated the path before me.

CHAPTER SIX

MIA BIANCHI

As I stepped away, the sound of laughter and clinking glasses faded behind me, replaced by the stillness of the night. A strange sensation clung to me like an unwelcome shadow, the feeling of being watched sending a shiver down my spine. I glanced back toward the glowing entrance of the gala, but nothing seemed out of place. The flickering candlelight and murmured conversations felt like a distant echo now, drowned out by the sharp clarity of my thoughts.

Romeo's gaze haunted me, its intensity burning through the crowd and leaving a mark I couldn't erase. It wasn't just a look—it was a silent confession, a whispered secret meant only for me. His eyes had felt like a caress, igniting something deep within me, a flicker of longing I hadn't dared to acknowledge until now.

What if Jamie finds out?

The thought tightened around my chest, a vice of guilt and panic. My crush on Romeo—Evra's brother—was a secret I could never admit, especially not to Jamie. Shoving the thought aside, I forced myself to focus on the task at hand: meeting Jamie. My mind churned with conflicting emotions, a chaotic storm of desire and loyalty that left me breathless.

When I arrived at Jamie's house, I hesitated on the welcome mat, my fingers poised above the doorbell. The soft chime echoed through the quiet night, amplifying the anticipation buzzing in the air. The door swung open, revealing Jamie's familiar face. His expression was a mix of apology and concern, the tension etched into the lines around his mouth.

"Hey," he said softly, pulling me into a brief embrace. His warmth enveloped me like a comforting blanket, but I couldn't shake the unease simmering just beneath the surface.

We settled onto his couch, the plush cushions swallowing us in their comfort. Jamie broke the silence first. "I'm sorry for yelling earlier," he began, his voice heavy with remorse. "I was out of line. I swear it won't happen again." His dark eyes searched mine, pleading for understanding.

I offered him a small smile, though my chest felt heavy with guilt. "It's okay, Jamie. I know you didn't mean it."

We talked for hours, the conversation drifting from work frustrations to dreams for the future. Laughter spilled out like sunlight breaking through clouds, momentarily lifting the tension between us. But no matter how much I tried to stay present, thoughts of Romeo lingered in the corners of my mind, a shadow I couldn't escape.

As I lay in bed later that night, the memory of Romeo's piercing gaze replayed in my mind like a haunting melody. His charm, his confidence, the spark in his eyes—it all pulled at me, a magnetic force I couldn't resist.

Evra arrived unannounced the next morning, her eyes sparkling with mischief as she stepped into my living room. "You look like you've seen a ghost," she teased, flopping onto the couch with her usual flair.

Before I could respond, she added, "Oh, by the way, my brother asked about Jamie."

Her tone was almost playful, but my stomach dropped. My voice came out strained, barely masking my anxiety. "What did you tell him?"

Evra smirked, waving a hand dismissively. "Relax, bella. I didn't say anything. It's not my place."

I exhaled, relief washing over me, but then she added, "Although... I wouldn't mind if you two dated."

I nearly choked on my coffee. "Evra, no!" I stammered, heat rushing to my cheeks.

Her laughter filled the room as she stood, grabbing her bag. "Don't act so shocked. You're both stubborn, passionate, and undeniably compatible. Think about it!"

I stared after her, stunned and flustered. Her words swirled relentlessly in my mind, planting seeds of possibility I didn't dare water. Could Romeo feel something for me?

That evening, as I worked through my tasks, a knock at the door startled me. I opened it to find Romeo standing there, his presence commanding, framed by the golden glow of the setting sun.

"Hey," he greeted with a smile that could melt glaciers. In his hands, he held a bouquet of exotic flowers and a small, elegantly wrapped box.

"I was in the neighborhood and thought I'd stop by," he said casually, but the warmth in his eyes told me this visit was anything but casual.

The fragrance of the flowers was intoxicating, wrapping around me like an embrace. My cheeks flushed as I took them. "You shouldn't have, Romeo."

He stepped inside, his gaze soft but intense. "Spero che ti piacciano i fiori, bella. Sono rari e bellissimi, proprio come te." (I hope you like the flowers, beautiful. They're rare and beautiful, just like you.)

For the next few hours, we lost ourselves in conversation. His stories, his laughter, and the way he looked at me—it all felt so easy, so natural.

But as the evening wore on, reality intruded. My parents would be home soon, and I knew they wouldn't approve of him being here.

"Romeo," I said softly, "you should go. My dad... he's very protective."

Understanding flickered in his eyes. He stepped closer, brushing a gentle kiss on the back of my hand. "Arrivederci, bella. Ci vediamo presto." (Goodbye, beautiful. We'll see each other soon.)

As I watched him walk away, my heart ached with longing and uncertainty. Romeo had ignited something in me, something I couldn't ignore. But I knew this was only the beginning of a journey that could change everything.

CHAPTER SEVEN

ROMEO GIUSEPPE

The dim light in my father's office cast long shadows across the room, creating a chiaroscuro that danced against the mahogany walls. The air was thick with the scent of cigar smoke, a fragrant haze that mingled with the aged leather of the furniture and the faint aroma of wood polish, creating an ambiance steeped in power and history.

He sat in his worn, oversized chair, the leather creaking softly as he leaned back, his face illuminated by the faint orange glow of the cigar as he tapped the ash into a crystal tray, the sound a muted punctuation in the oppressive silence.

Across from him, Luca, his trusted consigliere, leaned forward, his posture tense as if he were a coiled spring ready to unleash violence at a moment's notice. The weight of unspoken threats lingered in the air like a storm about to break.

"Luca," my father began, his voice cool and laced with steel, each word deliberate. "The Petrov situation needs to be handled. Their debt has run its course, and they need to be reminded who holds the power." His gaze was unwavering, each syllable a clear directive wrapped in authority.

Luca's expression hardened, the shadows dancing across his face reflecting years of loyalty and calculated violence. "Understood, boss," he replied, his voice low and steady. "We'll make sure they don't mistake silence for weakness." His words were a promise of impending consequences, his loyalty a blade ready to strike.

I stood nearby, the coldness of the room seeping into my bones as I listened quietly, waiting for the right moment to speak. This was my father's world—brutal, methodical, and unforgiving. But tonight, I had something personal to discuss, a divergence from the cold calculations that defined our lives.

Clearing my throat, I stepped forward, the weight of my thoughts heavy on my shoulders. "Father," I began, choosing my words with care as if navigating a minefield. "There's something else."

He turned toward me, his sharp gaze narrowing with interest, the weight of his attention pressing down like an anchor. "Speak."

"I've met someone—a girl named Mia," I began, my heart racing as I pushed forward. "Her family... they've been through a lot, and I think they deserve a break. The Bianchi family."

His brow furrowed at the mention, the name stirring recognition in the depths of his memory. "The Bianchi's... Marco and his wife. Once wealthy, once powerful, then left with nothing." He leaned back, taking a slow drag from his cigar, the smoke curling upward like a whisper of the past. "Marco trusted the system. He lost everything and now slaves away in construction while his wife is reduced to working as a cashier." His tone was devoid of pity, merely a recounting of facts that painted a grim picture of loss.

I nodded, feeling the respect I had for Mia and her family deepen with every detail he recounted.

"Why bring this to me?" my father asked, his gaze sharpening like the edge of a blade.

"I want to help them, to get closer to Mia," I said, my voice gaining strength, each word a step into uncharted territory. "Their resilience... I respect it. I want to be involved."

For a moment, he said nothing, his eyes studying me, weighing my sincerity against the backdrop of our reality. Then, a subtle smile tugged at the corners of his mouth, though he said nothing about our true legacy—the darkness we lived in. His silence was a message, carrying weight beyond words, a silent acknowledgment of the crossroads at which I stood.

Later That Evening

The softness of Mia's hand in mine was grounding, the warmth of her touch a soothing balm against the chill of my world. As we walked, her eyes searched mine, brimming with trust and vulnerability—two things I had long abandoned in my life. I marveled at the innocence that radiated from her, a stark contrast to the shadows that loomed just beyond our shared moments. She didn't know about the darkness that followed me, the truths I was sworn to keep hidden from her.

"Mia," I whispered, my voice low and steady, infused with an urgency that cut through the stillness. "I promise I'll help your family. You won't lose everything-not-not-not-not—not while I'm around."

Her eyes lingered on mine, filled with questions she didn't know how to articulate, an unspoken bond forming between us. For a fleeting moment, I wondered if she could sense the weight of the world I kept hidden from her. But her innocence remained intact, and I silently vowed it would stay that way.

The guilt gnawed at me, a relentless specter haunting my thoughts, knowing that while I wanted to help her, I was also keeping her in the dark. She didn't need to know the monsters lurking in the shadows of my life, the threats that loomed large over my every decision.

From the corner of my eye, I noticed my father standing in the distance, the faint glow of his cigar illuminating his figure like a beacon of authority. His sharp eyes took in everything—the closeness between Mia and me, the weakness he perceived in my desire to protect her.

The Conversation with My Father

Later, after Mia had gone, my father's voice echoed in the dimly lit room, a cold wind sweeping through the warmth we had shared.

"Romeo, this girl... she's making you weak." His tone was stern, an unwavering decree meant to cut through any semblance of doubt.

I turned to face him, my jaw clenched in defiance. "She's not a pawn, Father. She's more than that."

He studied me for a moment, the weight of his disappointment hanging in the air like a heavy fog. "You know the rules. Emotions cloud judgment. And in this world, we can't afford that." His voice held a coldness that chilled me, a reminder of the precarious balance we navigated daily.

"I won't let her be dragged into this," I replied, my voice firm, each word a vow I was desperate to uphold. "She doesn't need to know."

For the first time, my father's gaze softened, though the coldness of his words remained. "We'll see how long that lasts."

The challenge in his voice hung between us, a silent war brewing beneath the surface. I stood there, grappling with the tumult of emotions swirling in my chest, the weight of my responsibilities bearing down like a storm on the horizon.

CHAPTER EIGHT

MIA BIANCHI

The bustling halls of my third year at university greeted me with their usual energy, yet an unsettling feeling gnawed at the back of my mind, wrapping around me like a chilling mist. The air buzzed with the chatter of students rushing to classes, the scent of freshly brewed coffee and pastries wafting through the corridor, but I felt detached, as though I were merely a spectator in a world that buzzed with life.

It had been days since I received the letter informing me that my tuition had been mysteriously paid in full, and the shock still lingered, a bittersweet taste clinging to my tongue.

The weight of my rigorous course load should have been the only thing pressing down on me, but the unexpected meeting with the Registrar left me spiraling. An anonymous benefactor had covered my fees, and no amount of questioning could pry more information from the office staff. Their polite smiles and vague assurances only served to deepen my frustration. "Someone handled it," they said, but their eyes betrayed no further information.

I wandered through endless possibilities in my mind, each one darker than the last. My parents? No, they were struggling to keep afloat as it was, barely managing their bills while navigating the complexities of life. Evra, my best friend? Impossible—she was buried under her expenses, juggling her final year of law school and part-time work to make ends meet. The thought of an unknown benefactor stepping into my life to perform such a generous act without so much as an explanation left me with a heavy, unsettling feeling. What were their motives? What strings were attached?

Determined to unravel this mystery, I left the administration building and made my way to the university café, a cozy haven adorned with rustic wooden tables and the aroma of baked goods. The soft murmur of conversation and the clinking of cups created a familiar atmosphere, but it did little to calm my racing thoughts. I spotted Evra in our usual corner, her fingers dancing over her laptop's keyboard, her brow furrowed in concentration. As I slid into the chair beside her, my mind buzzed with questions, a storm of uncertainty raging within me.

"Evra, you won't believe what just happened," I began, my voice a mix of confusion and excitement. "Someone paid off all my school fees, and I have no idea who. The Registrar wouldn't tell me anything."
Evra's fingers froze mid-stroke, her eyes widening in surprise as if I had just revealed a secret she could hardly fathom. "Wait, what? That's insane! Who would do that?" Her voice rose slightly, drawing curious glances from nearby tables.

"I don't know," I muttered, shaking my head in frustration, my fingers fidgeting with the edge of the table. "But it's kind of unsettling, don't you think? Why would someone do something like that and not want me to know?" The words tumbled out, a mix of curiosity and dread swirling in my gut.

Evra's expression shifted from shock to curiosity, her tone dropping to a conspiratorial whisper, as if sharing a juicy secret. "Maybe it's a secret admirer. Someone who has a thing for you." Her eyes sparkled with mischief, and I could tell she was savoring the drama of the moment.

I scoffed, unable to suppress the laugh that escaped my lips. "You've been reading too many romance novels, Evra." I leaned back in my chair, attempting to dismiss the notion, but the idea of a secret admirer planted a seed of intrigue that began to take root in my mind.

She grinned, but I could see the wheels turning in her head, her curiosity piqued. Even though I brushed it off, the mystery weighed heavily on me, an anchor dragging me into deeper waters. Who would go to such lengths for me? What did they want in return?

The questions churned in my mind, refusing to be ignored even as I attempted to focus on lighter conversation with Evra. I sipped my coffee, the bitter warmth grounding me momentarily, but then she spoke again, her tone more hesitant this time, pulling me back into the storm of uncertainty.

"Mia, I think I know who might have done it."

My heart leaped into my throat, and I felt a jolt of adrenaline course through me. "Who?" I asked, leaning in closer, my pulse quickening.

Evra glanced around the café, her eyes darting to the few other patrons, as if checking to ensure no one else could overhear our conversation. She leaned in closer, her voice lowering to a whisper, thick with intrigue. "My brother, Romeo. He's been doing well for himself lately... and I think he wanted to help you out."

A wave of shock crashed over me, leaving me momentarily speechless. Romeo? I barely knew him beyond a few polite interactions and fleeting glances in the hallways. Why would he—someone so distant in my life—pay off such a huge debt for me?

"Romeo?" I repeated, disbelief flooding my voice, tinged with confusion. "Why would he do that?" I tried to comprehend the idea, but it felt like grasping at smoke.

Evra's expression grew more serious, her casual demeanor slipping away like a mask revealing something deeper. "I don't know for sure, but I've seen the way he looks out for people he cares about. I wouldn't be surprised if he saw this as a way to help." Her voice softened, sincerity shining in her eyes.

Gratitude mixed with confusion swirled inside me like a tempest, leaving me adrift in a sea of emotions. What could I possibly offer in return? Before I could articulate my thoughts further, Evra's tone shifted again, this time cautious, as if she were treading carefully on fragile ground.

"But Mia... if you ever cross paths with him again, just be careful, okay?" Her brow furrowed, concern etching deep lines across her forehead.

A frown creased my brow, instinctively wary of her warning. "Careful? What do you mean?" I searched her face for clues, my heart thrumming in my chest.

Evra hesitated, her expression troubled as she struggled to find the right words. "Romeo... he's intense. You might not fully understand the world he's in. I just want you to be sure—whatever he offers, whatever he does—be careful. Don't let him pull you into something you're not ready for."

Her words sent a chill through me, unsettling my already fragile sense of calm. I nodded slowly, though the confusion lingered like a heavy fog around my thoughts.

What kind of world was Romeo involved in that warranted such caution? And more importantly, why did he want to help me in the first place?

As I left the café, the vibrant chatter and laughter faded into the background, leaving only the weight of my unanswered questions pressing down on me. The mysterious benefactor—and Romeo's role in all of this— swirled in my mind like a storm that refused to dissipate. I took a deep breath, steeling myself against the uncertainty that lay ahead.

With each step, I couldn't shake the feeling that my life

had just taken a turn into uncharted territory, and I was both excited and terrified of what was to come.

CHAPTER NINE

ROMEO GIUSEPPE

The next day, as I moved through the bustling corridors of the family business, the weight of responsibility pressed down on me like a dark cloud. The air buzzed with muted conversations, and the clicking of polished shoes echoed against the marble floors, but my mind was elsewhere. Thoughts of Mia consumed me, each one more intoxicating than the last.

Despite my father's warnings and Mr. Bianchi's threats, I couldn't resist the overwhelming urge to send her gifts.

"Non posso resistere all'idea di farle sapere che mi importa," I muttered under my breath, the words a bittersweet mantra, a quiet rebellion against the surrounding chaos. ("I can't resist letting her know I care.") This was no fleeting thought; it had become a relentless need, a reminder that my heart still beat for her amid the turmoil of our families.

As I passed my father's office, the familiar scent of cigars and aged wood filled the air. The office was a shrine to my father's hard work, yet it felt like a gilded cage. He sat behind his desk, engulfed in a fortress of paperwork, each stack a testament to his pursuit of power and control. When he saw the determination in my face, his brow furrowed with concern.

He leaned back, exhaling a plume of smoke, the haze curling like a ghost. "I know how you feel, son," he said, his voice softening with nostalgia, a trace of longing. "When I wanted to marry your mother, my father had his concerns. But be careful, Romeo. Mr. Bianchi is not a man to be trifled with."

The words felt heavy, but I couldn't suppress a smirk, a flicker of defiance stirring inside me. "Sembra che sia una tradizione di famiglia, allora. Sfidare le probabilità per amore." ("Looks like it's a family tradition, then. Defying the odds for love.")

My father chuckled, his eyes briefly softening, but the weight of his warning lingered in the air. As the day wore on, I tried to focus on the family business, but the ache for Mia never left me. It gnawed at my resolve, a constant reminder of her absence.

Later, I found myself staring out of my office window, the city sprawling before me like a blur. "Mi manca tanto, papà," I whispered, my voice barely audible. ("I miss her so much, Dad.") The world outside was vibrant, alive, yet I felt a deep emptiness inside.

My father's face softened, but before he could respond, the door to my office burst open. Mr. Bianchi stormed in, fury radiating from him like an impending storm. The tension thickened instantly.

Without a word, he slammed a bundle of gifts onto my desk. The delicate wrapping, the colorful ribbons—they were a stark contrast to his fury. His eyes blazed with anger as he looked at me, a warning in every glance.

"Stay away from my daughter, Romeo. This is your last warning," he growled, his voice sharp and unforgiving. The room seemed to shrink around me, the silence suffocating. I met his gaze, unyielding, refusing to back down.

As he stormed out, my thoughts raced. I had to be with Mia—but how could I protect her from her father's wrath without endangering her? "Non mi arrenderò," I vowed silently, clenching my fists. ("I won't give up.")

Later, in a tense meeting, my mind kept drifting back to her. I muttered under my breath, frustrated and distracted, "Non posso smettere di pensare a lei." ("I can't stop thinking about her.")

After the meeting, I rushed to my father's office. "Papà, devo vederla," I said urgently, my voice thick with desperation. ("Dad, I need to see her.") The words tumbled out, desperate and raw.

He looked up at me, concern flickering in his eyes. "Romeo, be patient. We'll find a way, but for now, stay away from Mia." His voice was steady, but the weight of his words felt like chains around my chest.

"I know," I replied, but the struggle to resist was unbearable. "È così difficile resistere all'impulso di essere con lei." ("It's so hard to resist the urge to be with her.")

Days passed, then weeks, without a word from Mia. Doubt crept in, dark and relentless. Had she moved on? Forgotten about me? The uncertainty gnawed at me, threatening to consume me. "Non posso arrendermi," I whispered, clinging to the hope that one day we would be together. ("I can't give up.")

During a rare moment of solace, I spoke with Evra, my sister, my anchor. "Evra, non so cosa fare," I confessed, my heart heavy with longing. ("Evra, I don't know what to do.") "Mi manca tanto Mia." ("I miss Mia so much.")

Evra listened intently, her understanding gaze grounding me. "Romeo, stai facendo la cosa giusta. Dai tempo a Mia, e lei verrà da te." ("Romeo, you're doing the right thing. Give Mia time, and she'll come to you.") Her words, simple but full of weight, offered me the comfort I needed, like a light in the darkness.

"Grazie, Evra. Sei sempre stata la mia roccia." ("Thank you, Evra. You've always been my rock.") Her presence soothed me, but as I looked into her eyes, I saw something— hesitation, uncertainty. Something unspoken.

"Romeo, posso dirti una cosa?" Evra asked, her voice trembling with hesitation. ("Romeo, can I tell you something?")

I nodded, my heart racing. "Cosa è?" ("What is it?")

Her gaze lingered for a moment before she spoke. "Mia non ti dimentica, Romeo. Ma si sente in colpa per quello che sta succedendo." ("Mia hasn't forgotten you, Romeo. But she feels guilty about what's happening.") Her words hit me like a wave, but they also brought me a bittersweet sense of relief.

"Capisco," I murmured, the weight of her revelation sinking in. ("I understand.")

I tried to bury myself in work, but my thoughts kept wandering back to Mia. The ache never left, but I couldn't resist the urge to reach out to her.

Restlessness gnawed at me, urging me to break free from the confines of the office. I slipped outside into the bustling streets, hoping the fresh air would clear my mind. The world around me hummed with life, but my thoughts were consumed by Mia—the warmth of her smile, the softness of her touch, the ache of love caught between our families' feuds.

I would find a way to reach her, to bridge the divide between us. With every step, my resolve grew stronger. No matter what, love would triumph.

CHAPTER TEN

MIA BIANCHI

I still remember the day Romeo came to our house as if it were yesterday. His confident stride and charming smile made my heart skip a beat, but my father, Mr. Marco Bianchi, was not impressed at all. The front door swung open with a creak, and there he stood—an image of youthful charm with tousled hair that caught the light, eyes sparkling with mischief and a hint of something deeper.

"How dare you come to my house!" my father thundered, his face turning a deep shade of crimson with anger, his voice booming like a summer storm rolling through the hills. The air felt charged with tension, and I could almost hear the crackle of electricity. "You're not welcome here, Romeo. Stay away from my daughter!"

Romeo looked taken aback, his expression a mix of surprise and disappointment, but he nodded, shoulders slightly slumping as he turned to leave without uttering a word. The quiet thud of the door closing behind him resonated in the silence, leaving me feeling hollow and regretful. As I watched him go, guilt and embarrassment churned in my stomach, weighing heavy on my heart.

Later that evening, Evra came over, her expression sympathetic as she enveloped me in a tight embrace. The warmth of her friendship wrapped around me like a comforting blanket, making me feel momentarily safe from the chaos of my emotions. "Mia, I'm so sorry about what happened," she said softly, her voice laced with concern. "Your father can be... overprotective sometimes."

We retreated to my room, surrounded by the familiar comforts of my childhood—the walls adorned with posters of my favorite bands, and the air filled with the lingering scent of lavender from the candle flickering on my desk. Evra looked at me earnestly, her eyes pleading for me to give Romeo a chance. "He's been suffering, Mia. I've never seen him so smitten."

But doubt crept into my mind like a shadow, darkening my thoughts. "What about my father's warning?" I asked, a wave of uncertainty washing over me. "He was so angry, Evra. I've never seen him like that before."

Evra sighed, her fingers brushing my arm in a gesture that felt more protective than comforting. "I know," she replied gently, her voice soothing as she brushed a strand of hair behind my ear, her touch soft and reassuring. "But sometimes your father can be too much. He just wants to protect you. You're growing up, and you deserve to make your own choices."

Her words stirred something within me—a sense of rebellion against my father's rules, igniting a flicker of defiance in my heart. "Besides, Romeo is a great guy," Evra continued, her voice brightening, sparkling with enthusiasm. "He's kind, charming, and genuinely interested in you. Look, he got you these gifts."

With a flourish, Evra pulled out a box filled with beautiful trinkets and jewelry, each piece glimmering in the soft light. I gasped in surprise, my heart fluttering at the thought of him, the flutter of my emotions akin to the delicate wings of a butterfly caught in a gentle breeze.

"He begged me to give them to you, scared of your father's reaction," Evra confessed, her voice a conspiratorial whisper. "Please, Mia, don't tell your father that Romeo gave these to you. Let it be our little secret."

I nodded, excitement bubbling within me like a shaken soda as I tucked the gifts away, each item a token of Romeo's affection—glistening earrings and a delicate bracelet that sparkled with promise. The next morning, determination swelled in my chest, and I found myself standing in front of Romeo's mansion, the wrought iron gates looming before me, ready to confront the tangled mess of emotions I felt.

When Romeo met me in the garden, he looked more handsome than ever, sunlight dancing in his tousled hair like golden strands, his smile radiating warmth and charm. The garden was a vibrant tapestry of colors, blooming flowers swaying gently in the breeze, their sweet scent mingling with the fresh morning air. We strolled through the lush greenery, our footsteps crunching softly on the gravel path, the world around us falling away as we lost ourselves in conversation.

"Why are you doing all this, Romeo?" I asked, my voice firm despite the fluttering in my stomach, the weight of my curiosity pressing down on me like an anchor. "You know nothing about me."

His smile broadened, eyes crinkling at the corners, sparkling with sincerity. "I know enough, Mia. I know you're kind, intelligent, and beautiful. And I want to get to know you better."

A rush of emotions surged through me, overwhelming and intoxicating, like a sweet melody resonating in my heart. The moment felt electric, and before I could think, I stepped forward and kissed him, the spark igniting a flame that spread through my veins. But he gently pulled away, his expression serious, the moment shifting like a sudden gust of wind.

"Mia, wait," he said softly, his voice filled with a mixture of longing and caution, his gaze piercing into my soul. "I want to do this right. I want to court you, to get to know you properly. Will you give me three months? If you don't want me after that, I'll leave you alone."

His words took me aback, stirring a mix of excitement and uncertainty within me, like a storm brewing on the horizon. I felt my heart race at the prospect, yet fear tugged at my mind. His request felt so intense, so serious. Three months? Could I commit to something like that? The mere thought of his words made the storm in my chest intensify, and before I could think through the consequences, I stepped forward again and kissed him fiercely, our lips crashing together in a whirlwind of emotion, the kiss electrifying as it lingered, full of promise and urgency.

It felt like time stood still, each second stretching into eternity as the world faded away. A wave of exhilaration crashed over me, but when I pulled away, I saw surprise etched on his face, the realization of the moment reflecting in his eyes. I could tell he hadn't expected my reaction, and for a moment, it made me question myself. Why had I kissed him like that? What had come over me?

"Mia, I..." he began, his voice trailing off, but I couldn't bear to hear him finish. Instead, I turned and fled, embarrassment flooding through me like a tidal wave. I didn't stop until I reached my room, slamming the door shut behind me, my heart racing like a wild stallion, each beat echoing in my ears.

Leaning against the door, I tried to catch my breath, grappling with the whirlwind of emotions that had just consumed me. Why had I kissed him like that? I felt like I had lost control, yet a part of me knew I couldn't avoid Romeo forever. I needed to face him, to talk it out. For now, I just leaned against the door, trying to calm my racing heart and make sense of everything that had happened.

After a moment, I ventured outside, allowing the fresh air and warm sunshine to wash over me, cleansing my thoughts. With each step, clarity began to settle within me, guiding me like a beacon. I turned a corner and found myself in front of my house, my feet seemingly leading me home without conscious thought.

Standing outside, I looked up at the familiar windows and doors, memories flooding my mind like a gentle tide. I walked inside, closing the door behind me, enveloped in comforting silence. The tranquility of my childhood home washed over me like a warm embrace, wrapping me in its familiar scent, the soft hues of the walls soothing my frazzled nerves.

I took a deep breath, feeling the tension in my body ease, before making my way toward the kitchen. My feet creaked softly on the floorboards as I moved, the house empty but filled with echoes of laughter and love that danced in the air.

Upon entering the kitchen, the faint scent of freshly baked cookies wafted through the air, wrapping around me like a nostalgic hug. My mom must have baked some earlier, I thought, a smile tugging at my lips as I recalled the warmth of her presence.

I walked over to the counter, spotting a plate of still-warm chocolate chip cookies accompanied by a note: "Mia, hope you're doing okay. Love you, Mom." The handwriting was delicate and loving, each loop and curve a reminder of her nurturing spirit.

Warmth filled my heart, knowing my mother was thinking of me, her love a constant presence in my life. I grabbed a cookie and took a bite, savoring the gooey chocolate and crunchy edges—like a hug in cookie form, comforting and sweet.

As I sat in my room, trying to process everything that had transpired, confusion and uncertainty loomed over me like dark clouds, heavy and foreboding. I had been dating Jamie Evans for three years, and I shouldn't be feeling this way about another guy.

But I couldn't deny the connection I felt with Romeo, the pull of attraction strong and undeniable. Just then, my phone buzzed, interrupting my thoughts like a jolt of electricity. It was Evra.

"Girl, what's going on?" she asked, concern lacing her voice, her intuition sharp as ever.

Sighing, I attempted to articulate my tangled feelings, each word a struggle, as if I were trying to navigate a labyrinth. "I kissed Romeo, Evra. And I don't know what to do."

Her excitement was palpable, radiating through the screen like warmth from a fire, brightening my mood even if just a little. "Yaaas, finally! You deserve so much better than Jamie's toxic butt. Break up with him and go for Romeo!"

I laughed, a mix of emotions swirling within me, the tension beginning to ease, her exuberance infectious. "It's not that simple, Evra. I've been with Jamie for three years. What about all the time we've spent together?"

"Mia, you can't ignore how you feel," she replied, her voice firm yet supportive, grounding me in the whirlwind of my thoughts. "You deserve to be happy. If Jamie is making you miserable, it's time to walk away."

As the truth of her words settled in, I knew she was right. This was my life, my choice, and I couldn't let anyone dictate how I felt, especially not Jamie. It was time to confront the reality of my situation and reclaim my happiness, regardless of the consequences.

That evening, as I paced my room, anxiety coiled within me like a tightly wound spring, my heart pounding in my chest as I rehearsed what I would say to Jamie. I needed to be brave, to stand my ground, and to break free from the chains that had bound me for so long.

The air was thick with anticipation, each breath a reminder of the confrontation that lay ahead. I couldn't let fear dictate my life anymore. It was time to face the truth and embrace my future.

CHAPTER ELEVEN

ROMEO GIUSEPPE

As we step out of the café, I grasp Mia's hand, an electrifying rush of excitement and nervousness surging through me. The warm evening air wraps around us, scented with fresh pastries and coffee, heightening my determination. I have to make her mine, and I'll go to any length to achieve that.

I've been paying attention to her, learning the little things that make her smile. With her birthday approaching, I've spent weeks crafting the perfect surprise. Every detail is planned.

The day arrives, and I lead her to her favorite Italian restaurant—rustic décor, candlelit tables, and the air alive with laughter and the clinking of wine glasses. It's intimate, the perfect setting for what I have in mind.

We indulge in rich pasta and savory sauces, stealing glances at her as she savors every bite. The conversation flows effortlessly, full of teasing and flirting, building our connection.

After dinner, I signal the waiter. He wheels in a cart, elegantly presenting a stunning cake beneath the soft glow of the lights. My heart swells as I drop to one knee, a velvet box trembling in my hand.

"Happy birthday, Mia," I say, my voice thick with emotion. "I wanted to make this day special for you."

I open the box, revealing a diamond necklace that sparkles like a distant star. Her eyes widen in disbelief, a moment suspended in time.

But the real surprise is outside. I take her hand, guiding her into the cool night air. Beneath the starlit sky, a brand-new Rolls-Royce Dawn gleams, wrapped in a bright red bow.

"This is for you, my love," I say, handing her the keys. "I want you to know how much you mean to me."

Her eyes sparkle as she takes the keys, disbelief and joy mixing on her face.

"Romeo, this is too much," she whispers, her voice barely above a breath.

"You deserve it," I reply, my heart swelling with pride. "You deserve the best, and I'm going to give it to you."

As we settle into the plush leather seats, I steal glances at her. But when we pull away, I notice the flicker of guilt and uncertainty in her eyes. I know Jamie's shadow still haunts her, and it gnaws at me. But I won't let him take her from me.

"Hey, baby," I murmur, trying to ease her fears. "I don't care about him. This is about us."

My gaze locks on hers, my voice steady, filled with unspoken sadness. "You don't need to feel guilty. You're not married, and your toxic ex can't stop us. What God has joined together, no man—especially not your ex—can tear apart."

I pause, gripping the wheel, the tension in my muscles palpable. "But if he tries, I won't hesitate to deal with him. I'd wipe him off this planet without a second thought."

Mia laughs, startled, thinking I'm joking, but I'm not. "Now that you're mine, I'm going to treat you like the queen you are," I continue. "The way Jamie treated you wasn't how a real man does."

I glance at her again, seeing the fear mixed with uncertainty, yet beneath it, there's a flicker of attraction, a glimmer of hope.

"Every day brings your ex closer to his grave," I say, my voice chilling with dark intent. "I haven't acted yet because of you, Mia. But I wouldn't hesitate if I had to."

Taking a deep breath, emotion floods through me, raw and vulnerable. "I would burn the world for you. To show you how much I love you."

Her eyes lock with mine, and I can see her processing everything. Her mind races to understand the depth of my feelings for her. Shock, fear, and awe mix in her expression, and I know she's trying to make sense of me—of us.

"Romeo, I..." she begins, her voice a whisper filled with longing.

I stop her, my voice low and urgent. "Don't say anything, Mia. Just know that I'm all in. I'll do whatever it takes to make you happy, to keep you safe."

I pause, my heart laid bare. "I know I'm not perfect. But I promise, I'll never hurt you like Jamie did. I'll never make you feel like you're not enough."

Tears glisten in her eyes as emotions swirl—love, fear, confusion. I reach out, brushing a strand of hair from her face, my thumb gently caressing her cheek.

"Hey, baby," I whisper, my voice soft and reassuring. "It's okay. I've got you. I'm not letting go."

As we drive through the city, the lights shimmering like stars, the weight of our shared moments binds us closer. I can feel her heart caught between her past and the future,

I promise. I'll fight for her, against Jamie, against any fear or uncertainty that dares to come between us.

This is just the beginning. I'll do everything in my power to make her feel loved, cherished, and safe. Because to me, she's worth every sacrifice.

CHAPTER TWELVE

MIA BIANCHI

I was still reeling from Romeo's words: *"I can fucking burn the world for you to show you how much I love you."* His intensity both scared and captivated me, igniting a fire in my veins that I'd never known. As we drove away, the city skyline fading into the distance, his grip on my hand tightened—an unspoken promise, an invisible thread that drew us closer.

"I have one more stop to make," he said, his voice laced with excitement, his eyes gleaming like polished obsidian under the dashboard lights.

Before I could ask, he turned the Rolls-Royce onto a side street, and a neon sign flickered to life in the dusk: *"Amico's Tattoo Parlor."* The vibrant colors against the night sent a thrill of curiosity rushing through me.

Romeo smiled, a boyish grin spreading across his face.
"I've been coming here for years. Amico's an old friend,"
he explained, nostalgia warming his voice.

He pulled into a parking spot, the engine purring softly as
it settled. A flutter of anticipation filled my chest. What
was this all about? My mind raced with possibilities.

Stepping out of the car, the crisp night air wrapped around
us, invigorating. The tattoo parlor door creaked open, and
the bell above jingled softly. Amico looked up, his grin
widening at the sight of Romeo. His tattooed arms
glistened under the warm light, telling tales of life and
adventure.

Sitting down, Romeo turned to me, his gaze intense. "Mia,
from the moment I met you, I knew you were different.
You're the one I want to spend my life with," he declared,
his words a quiet storm in my chest.

He took my hand, his warmth radiating through me. "I
want to make it permanent, to show you how much I love
you," he whispered, his voice reverent, like a sacred vow.

"Romeo, my man! What brings you here?" Amico boomed, his grin deepening, his voice familiar and warm.

Romeo's gaze locked with mine, filled with determination. "I want a tattoo of Mia's name across my chest. In bold letters," he said, the weight of his words hanging in the air.

Amico raised an eyebrow. "Whoa, serious? You want her name?"

Romeo nodded, his jaw set, unwavering. "Across my chest. In bold letters."

Amico whistled. "That's a statement. You sure you're ready for that?"

"I've never been more sure of anything in my life," Romeo replied, and I felt the truth of his words seep deep into my bones.

A shiver ran down my spine, a mix of exhilaration and fear. Amico, seeing the resolve in Romeo's eyes, nodded. "Alright, let's do this." The tattoo machine buzzed to life, its hum filling the room like a heartbeat.

I watched as the needle pierced Romeo's skin, leaving ink and blood—an act of love and sacrifice. Each line etched into him felt like a promise. The pain, the beauty—everything was for me.

"Romeo, are you sure this is worth it?" I whispered, concern tightening my chest.

He smiled, a warmth that soothed me. "Every moment of pain is worth it if it means I can show you how much I love you."

"Romeo, look at me," I whispered, my voice trembling with desperation.

His eyes met mine, filled with a mix of pain and adoration. "I'm okay, amore mio," he whispered, his voice a soothing balm. "I'm exactly where I want to be."

Minutes passed, each one stretching into eternity as I watched him endure, my heart aching. Finally, Amico stepped back, admiring his work.

"It's done," he announced, his voice filled with pride. Romeo stood, his chest bare and vulnerable, my name etched across his skin—a permanent mark of devotion.

Tears prickled at the corners of my eyes as I traced the letters with my fingertip, my emotions surging.

"Romeo, it's beautiful," I whispered, my voice thick with gratitude.

He smiled, his eyes crinkling with joy. "You're beautiful, Mia. And now, you're mine forever," he declared, his voice heavy with conviction.

His words wrapped around me, pulling me closer as he embraced me, his chest pressing against mine. I could feel the steady thrum of his heart, a rhythm that echoed my own.

"I love you, Mia," he whispered against my ear, the words a declaration of intent.

My heart skipped, warmth flooding me as I pulled back, tears shimmering in my eyes. "Romeo, I... I care about you so much," I stammered, my voice trembling.

His face softened, understanding in his eyes. "I know, amore mio," he whispered, his tone tender. "You don't have to say it yet. I just need you to know how I feel."

I nodded, a mix of happiness, fear, and uncertainty swirling within me. But as I looked into his eyes—so sincere and warm—I knew I was exactly where I was meant to be, ready to dive into the unknown depths of our shared journey.

CHAPTER THIRTEEN

MIA BIANCHI

As I nodded, a whirlwind of emotions surged within me, each one more powerful than the last. Romeo's face lit up with a warm, infectious smile as he pulled me close, his chest still bare from the tattoo. "Let's get out of here," he whispered, his voice a low murmur that sent a thrill down my spine.

We left the tattoo parlor, walking hand in hand through the quiet streets. The night air was sweet with blooming flowers, the distant hum of city life wrapping us in intimacy. Moonlight danced on the pavement, spotlighting our connection. Romeo led me to a small café, where we settled into a cozy window-side table. As he ordered us coffee, I found myself captivated by his stories of childhood mischief, each tale laced with a deeper, unspoken meaning.

But beneath the ease of our conversation, a dark whisper stirred—a nagging feeling that Romeo might be hiding something from me, a secret that could shatter this fragile moment. Despite the guilt tugging at me—lingering thoughts of Jamie and whether I was moving too fast—I couldn't resist Romeo. Everything about him felt effortless and intoxicating, like something I shouldn't touch but couldn't resist.

He smiled, brushing his hand against mine. That simple touch sent a jolt through me. "I'm sorry," I whispered, pulling away, anxiety knotting my stomach. "I don't know if I'm ready for this."

His eyes softened, radiating tenderness. Leaning in, he spoke with gentle conviction. "We don't have to rush, Mia. I just want to be with you." His words calmed my storm of uncertainty, and for a moment, I allowed myself to believe I could find happiness again.

As we finished our coffee and stepped back into the night, hope flickered in my chest. But guilt continued to gnaw at me. Was I moving too fast? Was this just a rebound?

The following night, Romeo took me to a high-end club, where we let go, dancing and drinking as if time didn't exist. The energy was electric, the music syncing with my racing heart. In his arms, I was lost, surrendering to the whirlwind. But when our lips brushed together, Romeo pulled back, his gaze serious. "Not like this," he whispered, his breath a warm caress. "I won't take advantage of you."

Disappointment flared, but the desire in his eyes burned brighter, and he pulled me into a kiss that was fierce and wild. As the night wore on, I knew I was lost in him—lost in this magnetic pull. I didn't care about the consequences; I only wanted Romeo.

Later, at his mansion, the intensity between us remained electric, but there was something more—a protectiveness that made me feel safe amidst the chaos. "Mia," he whispered, his voice thick with emotion, "stay with me tonight. Please."

My heart raced as I nodded, fully aware of the line I was crossing, but I couldn't resist him any longer. In his arms, I finally felt where I belonged.

As we collapsed onto the couch, the realization of what we were doing hit me—a reminder of my untouched innocence. But with Romeo, everything felt different. I was ready to dive into the passion simmering between us.

Romeo hesitated, sensing my inner conflict, but the desire in his eyes mirrored mine. With one final kiss, we gave in, succumbing to the passion we had denied for too long. The surrounding air crackled with intensity, and in that moment, I knew there was no turning back.

"I wish that I could fuck you so hard right now." "But I wouldn't mind, though," he said huskily.

His hands found my wet thong as he brushed his fingers roughly against my pussy. I knew that he wanted to be gentle, but I didn't want to be gentle.

I wanted a very rough and hard fucking. I moaned loudly, as his fingers went inside me, rubbing my clit.

I knew that I masturbated but it wasn't this good with the way, he fucked me. He was a man of experience.

My thoughts trailed off as I gazed up at Romeo, my mind foggy with desire. I had been about to say something, but the words slipped away, lost in the depths of his piercing eyes. He was older, wiser, and infinitely more experienced than I was.

The years between us seemed to stretch out like a vast, unbridgeable chasm, a reminder of the secrets he kept, the stories he could tell, and the pleasures he could teach me.

His eyes seemed to hold a world of knowledge, a deep understanding of the desires that drove us both.

I felt like a novice, an innocent initiate, standing at the threshold of a mysterious realm, with Romeo as my guide.

The thought sent a shiver down my spine, a thrill of anticipation mixed with a hint of fear.

What was I getting myself into? And yet, I couldn't help but be drawn to him, like a moth to a flame, helpless to resist the allure of his experience, his passion, and his promise.

"Mia, sei la mia vita, la mia anima, la mia tutto. Mia, you're my life, my soul, my everything. La tua bellezza è la mia ossessione. Your beauty is my obsession", he said.

The sound of his voice was like a whispered secret, a gentle breeze that rustled the leaves of my soul. The words themselves were laced with a subtle seduction, a velvet-wrapped temptation that beckoned me closer.

Each syllable was a delicate brushstroke on the canvas of my heart, painting a picture of longing and desire.

As I heard the familiar phrase, my heart stumbled, like a dancer missing a step, and then skipped a beat, like a stone cast into a still pond, sending ripples of excitement through my very being.

It was as if my heart had been waiting, anticipating the sound of his voice, and when it came, it was like a key turning in a lock, unleashing a torrent of emotions.

The words themselves were a siren's call, a tantalizing promise of pleasure and passion, a whispered assurance that all my deepest desires would be fulfilled.

His voice was the devil's own, tempting me with sweet nothings, drawing me in with a subtle persuasion that was impossible to resist. And I, helpless and enthralled, was powerless to do anything but surrender to the allure of his words.

His breath caressed my skin, warm and sultry, like a gentle summer breeze on a Tuscan vineyard.

The scent of rich, full-bodied wine wafted from his lips, reminiscent of a fine Italian Merlot or Cabernet Sauvignon.

The aroma was intoxicating, making my head spin with desire. As he leaned in closer, the fragrance of his breath enveloped me, transporting me to the rolling hills of Italy.

I could almost taste the subtle notes of oak, vanilla, and dark fruit on his lips, like a sip of a luxurious wine.

His breath was a sensual delight, a prelude to the passion that awaited us. It was as if the essence of Italy itself had been distilled into his kiss, leaving me breathless and yearning for more.

This was the precipice, the moment of truth. I stood at the edge of destiny, where the path behind me was shrouded in uncertainty, and the road ahead was veiled in promise.

The choice was mine to make: to turn back, or to surrender to the unknown. But as I gazed into Romeo's eyes, burning with intensity and desire, all reason and doubt melted away.

His gaze was a siren's call, beckoning me to surrender to the depths of his passion. The surrounding air vibrated with tension, like the quiet before a storm, as if the very universe held its breath in anticipation.

In this moment, I knew what I truly wanted. I wanted the heat of Romeo's touch, the taste of his lips, the whispered promises in my ear.

I wanted the thrill of the unknown, the rush of adrenaline as we danced on the edge of fate. I wanted him, and him alone.

With a sense of reckless abandon, I let go of my fears, my doubts, my inhibitions. I let go of everything, except for the desire that burned within me.

And as I fell into his arms, I knew that I was embracing my fate and surrendering to the love that would consume us both. Romeo had removed his clothing without me realizing it. And helped me to discard mine. I was just left with my lingerie on.

He had slid my thong down to my ankles as he shifted my legs to have a good look at my pussy.

Feeling slightly embarrassed. I tried closing my legs, but Romeo roughly opened them.

"Don't close it," he ordered me.

"Daddy, needs to get a close look at that yummy pussy, he is about to eat."

My pussy clenched tightly as he spoke those words. I was deeply and utterly aroused. He leaned forward and gave my pussy a slap which wasn't supposed to turn me on than I was.

It was a mixture of pain and pleasure, and I did enjoy it, and I wished for him to do it again. He grew more aggressive as he kept spanking my pussy.

I gasped as my pussy tightened and ached with pleasure. And all I imagined were those long and thick fingers inside me and making me come so hard.

Desire for my intake pulsed deep inside my core, and my pussy clenched and ached with a wanton need. I hated the way he teased me.

Still upset, Romeo began spanking my thighs and continued to torture my pussy with spankings.

"What do you need, little girl?" he purred and asked me.

"You", I hoarsely said.

"But someone has been naughty, haven't they?" He asked me.

"Yes," I answered.

"Tell me what do you want and I will give it to you," he teased and asked.

"So, frustrated", I pleaded that it was him.

"Please fuck me, Papi," I begged Romeo like a whore, despite being too drunk and turned on.

Romeo freed his cock from his tracks, and what I saw made me question my decision. I wondered if that enormous cock would fit inside me.

I knew that it was going to hurt as hell. One, I am a virgin, and two, his thick girth. But that turned me on, that it left all thinking proportions of my brain.

His naked cock had made my inner walls to leak, as I imagined him sliding in and out of me and fucking hard as I wanted.

"Do you like what you see, my sweetest angel?" he asked. But I couldn't help but moan.

I loved what I saw, and there was no denying of such. I spread my legs wider and revealed all to him. He growled, as he lined his cock against my folds.

"Come on, darling, one more time, what do you need daddy to do for you?" he ordered me.

"I need you to fuck", but before I could complete the remaining sentence.

Romeo slammed his cock inside me, and my pussy quivered with excitement. It hurt as hell, as he slowly fucked me and I growled in pain as he continued fucking me.

"Please, baby, be still". With time, the pain would subside," he pleaded with me, as he agonizingly slid in and out of me.

My greedy pussy took inch and every girth of his, as I was a wet and needy virgin whore and I knew that the next day, my pussy would be well used and sore.

He was so huge, and despite it hurting. It felt really good. And I couldn't escape his girth, and I never wanted to. I whimpered and moaned as he slid inside me.

My body was trembling as I came hard, as he thrust harder. My body revolted as he fucked me so good with his enormous size, as if there were a switch.

Each thrust hurt and was rougher than the last one. His fingers wrapped around my neck, claiming me as his. Nothing mattered but that cock inside me. He slid in and out with an incredible force.

Making my tits shake with each rough thrust. Before I knew it, my inner walls spasmed around his cock.

I writhed underneath him, my orgasm rising higher and higher with each peak.

"Oh god, I am fucking going to come," I screamed out loudly.

As the words tumbled out of my mouth, my voice slurred and slow, like a gentle stream meandering through a moonlit garden. The room around me began to blur and fade, like a watercolor painting in the rain, as the weight of the wine and the warmth of Romeo's embrace conspired against me.

My eyelids grew heavy, like velvet curtains drawn down by an invisible hand, as I felt myself succumbing to the sweet surrender of sleep.

The sound of Romeo's voice, low and soothing, was the last thing I remembered, a gentle lullaby that wrapped itself around my heart and rocked me into oblivion.

In that fleeting moment, I was aware of nothing else but the sensation of being cradled in Romeo's arms, my head nestled in the crook of his shoulder, my body surrendering to the warmth and safety of his embrace.

The world outside receded, and all that remained was the gentle rise and fall of his chest, the whisper of his breath in my ear, and the sweet, sweet darkness that claimed me as its own.

Romeo did come inside me, filling me up with his semen.

CHAPTER FOURTEEN

ROMEO GIUSEPPE

As I stirred awake, the remnants of last night's revelry still swirling in my mind, I noticed Mia attempting to slip quietly out of bed. The soft rustling of the sheets drew my attention, and before she could make her escape, I gently grasped her wrist.

"Hey, it's okay," I murmured, my voice low and soothing, like a soft lullaby breaking the silence of dawn.

She froze, her wide, uncertain eyes meeting mine. We both knew the previous night had been filled with intoxicating passion and heady excitement. I remembered every moment—the electric tension between us, the way her body had quivered beneath mine. Sitting up, the morning light spilled into the room, illuminating the scene around us, casting a warm glow that made everything feel surreal. That's when I noticed the bloodstains on the sheets, stark against the pristine white fabric—a stark reminder of the gravity of the night.

My heart raced as the realization hit me—Mia had been a virgin. The first man she had ever been with, and perhaps, the only one.

A complex swirl of emotions surged within me: shock, pride, and a profound sense of responsibility. She wasn't just another woman; she was someone I wanted to protect, to cherish with everything I had.

"Mia," I began, shifting to face her fully. She looked down, avoiding my gaze as if it were a shield against the weight of reality. "You don't need to feel embarrassed. I... I didn't know you'd never been with anyone before."

Her cheeks flushed with color, and she averted her eyes, clearly uncomfortable with the vulnerability of the moment. "I didn't mean for it to happen like this," she murmured, her voice barely above a whisper, trembling with uncertainty.

Gently, I turned her face toward mine, cradling her chin in my hand. "Last night was special. You chose me to be your first, and that means everything to me." My voice was tender, like the soft caress of the morning breeze, as I brushed my thumb softly against her cheek. "I'll never forget it."

Mia's eyes glistened with unshed tears, her lower lip trembling as she struggled to process the whirlwind of emotions swirling around us. "It just felt right, Romeo. I don't know why, but... it did."

I nodded, understanding washing over me like a wave. "It felt right to me, too, bella." Leaning forward, I pressed a gentle kiss to her forehead, wanting to reassure her that everything between us had changed—but for the better.

To break the tension, I decided to prepare breakfast. Leaving her in the room, I moved to the kitchen, determined to make something that would bring a smile to her face. Cracking a few eggs into a bowl, I whisked them with practiced ease, humming an Italian tune under my breath, letting the melody lift my spirits. The rich scent of espresso soon filled the air, mingling with the buttery aroma of cornetti I had baked.

"Buongiorno, bella," I called out as she emerged from the bedroom, her hair tousled and wild from sleep, an enchanting sight that made my heart flutter.

My heart swelled at the sight of her—so raw, so vulnerable, yet undeniably beautiful. "How are you feeling?" I asked, setting the table with care, placing each item as if it were a delicate treasure.

Mia hesitated, then offered a shy smile, her cheeks still tinged with color. "A little embarrassed," she admitted, taking a seat, the unease lingering in her voice.

Pouring her a cup of espresso, I added just the right amount of sugar, watching her as I did, eager to see her reaction.

"There's no need to be," I said gently, my voice wrapped in sincerity. "I'm honored, Mia. Truly."

Her eyes sparkled as they met mine, a hint of gratitude shining through like the dawn breaking over the horizon. "Thank you, Romeo. For everything."

We ate in comfortable silence, the moment between us delicate and intimate. After we finished, I reached over, brushing a strand of hair behind her ear, my voice husky with emotion. "Ti amo, Mia," I whispered, letting the words hang in the air, heavy with meaning.

Her breath caught, and she looked down, clearly overwhelmed by the weight of my confession. "Romeo... I care about you, too. But this is all so much... I just need time."

I nodded, my heart aching for her as if it were made of glass. "Take all the time you need, mia amore. I'm not going anywhere."

After breakfast, I led Mia to the bathroom, where I had drawn a warm bath infused with lavender, its calming scent filling the air, inviting her to unwind. "Relax," I whispered as I helped her into the tub, taking my time washing her hair and gently massaging her scalp, hoping to make her feel safe and cherished, cocooned in warmth.

Once she was wrapped in a soft towel, I led her to the bedroom, where a plush robe awaited her, its fabric soft and inviting. "Feeling better?" I asked, my heart swelling with affection as I took in her serene expression.

"Si, grazie, Romeo," she replied softly, her voice laced with warmth.

"Prego," I said, my heart full. "Now, let me show you around the house."

I took her hand, leading her through the spacious rooms, pointing out my favorite art pieces and sharing stories from my life, each word a thread weaving us closer together. As we wandered into the garden, Mia's face lit up with wonder at the blooming flowers, sunlight casting a golden glow over everything, making her look radiant.

"This is beautiful, Romeo," she whispered, her voice full of awe, a melody to my ears.

I smiled, pride swelling within me like a rising tide. "I'm glad you like it, bella. This is my sanctuary."

As we reached the balcony, the view of the city sprawled out before us, breathtaking in its beauty, I could see the tension ease from her body as she took in the sight. But even in that moment, I couldn't shake the possessive urge that stirred within me, a primal instinct whispering that she was mine.

"From now on, you're mine," I said, my voice low and filled with conviction, a promise etched in the air between us.

Mia turned to me, her eyes wide with emotion, a storm of feelings swirling within their depths. "I'm yours, Romeo. Forever."

Her words sent a thrill through me, igniting a fire deep within my soul. I pulled her close, our lips meeting in a soft kiss, sealing the promise between us. As I gazed into her eyes, I knew this was just the beginning of something deeper, something that would change us both forever.

Yet, beneath the surface, a primal desire flickered within me, overwhelming and raw. The urge to possess her, to claim her entirely, tugged at my soul, a potent longing that refused to be ignored. My thoughts spiraled into a haze of need and yearning, visions of taking her in ways that left no doubt of my ownership.

But I held back, taming the beast within, savoring the sweet agony of restraint. The air thickened with tension, and the silence between us hummed with unspoken promises, each heartbeat echoing the depth of my desire.

Mia's eyes sparkled with mischief, her lips curling into a sly smile, as if she knew the depths of my desire and was determined to tease me further, drawing me in closer.

And I, helpless to resist, was drawn in—a moth to the flame, unable to escape the allure of her presence, the intoxicating pull of our connection.

With every glance from her seductive eyes, I felt the heat of desire swell within me. My thoughts were consumed with the image of sliding in and out of her, knowing I was the first and, I vowed, the last man to ever claim her.

As I wrapped my arms around her waist, pulling her closer, an overwhelming sense of pride and gratitude surged through me. I thanked the heavens for bringing her into my life, for entrusting me with the gift of her affection, my heart racing with each pulse of connection.

I held her tightly, as if I could shield her from the world, the softness of her curves pressing against me, her body fitting against mine like a second skin, a perfect match in the chaos of life.

Unable to resist the temptation to explore the beauty hidden beneath her robe, I undid a few buttons, my fingers brushing against her skin, gazing at the gorgeous curve of her cleavage that lay revealed.

Her chest pressed against the balcony railing, the cool night air caressing her exposed skin. Moonlight danced across her features, illuminating the gentle slope of her neck, the softness of her lips. I was captivated by her beauty, my heart swelling with emotion, desire burning brighter with every passing moment. In that intimate embrace, time stood still, a frozen tableau of longing and love.

I wanted her not just as a lover but as my own, to claim her wholly, to explore the depths of our connection, to cherish every moment we shared. The memory of our passionate night sent waves of longing through me, fueling an insatiable hunger that could not be quelled.

And in that moment, I knew I would do anything to keep her, to cherish her, to explore the depths of our connection, to make her feel as treasured as she truly was.

Mia was mine, and I would protect her with everything I had. I took a nipple into my mouth, sucking it like her Papi searching for her milk.

I lost all irrational thinking and sucked it like I was hungry for her. I satisfied her by giving the other nipple the treatment that it deserved.

I reached down, holding her ass cheeks hard and giving each one of them. The spanking they deserved. She moaned as she loved what I had done to her.

I moved my fingers down to her cunt, where I found a soaking Mia. I smirked as I slid my finger in. And fucking shit, did that tighten around it.

She had a fucking tight vice and I loved how it refused to let my fingers go. I licked her neck, tasting the sweetness of her skin.

As she kept getting off on my fingers. But one thing she didn't know was that I was in charge here and not her.

"Daddy, please," she begged me like a sweetest whore.

That was what she was for me. My precious whore and I owned all of it. I was so fed up with all the teasing that I was doing to her.

Then, I decided that it was time for her to get that whore's treatment from my cock. I pushed her legs apart, revealing everything to me.

In that moment, I didn't care about discretion, about subtlety. I wanted to claim her, to mark her as mine, to make it clear that she was off-limits to all others.

She was my possession, my treasure, my heart. And I was hers, solely and completely. As her cries grew louder, more insistent, I felt a surge of pride, of ownership.

I was the one who had unleashed this passion, who had awakened this fire within her.

And I was determined to be the only one to ever extinguish it. Amid her screams, I whispered a single word, a claim of ownership, a promise of forever:

"Mine." And in that moment, I knew that we were bound, irrevocably, irretrievably. She was mine, and I was hers. No one else existed.

Only us. Only our love. I slammed hard into her, as I pulled her hips closer to take me deeply, and Mia moaned with pleasure and excitement. Her eyes rolling and she writhing in pleasure, as she kept coming to no counts.

I held her hips as I pounded her hard and she still wanted more, as she begged me to fuck her hard. Who was I to deny such an obligation? I fucked her, while we kissed. Us going wild in the moment.

"Yes, Papi," she said. "Please fuck me hard and fuck your little whore harder", she pleaded with me.

And I answered. As we could hear the loud squishing noises of our fucking. Slamming my cock hard into her wet cunt. Slapping her ass with each thrust taken. Due to the tightness of her pussy and the times, Mia had come.

I increased my speed as any moment now, I was going to come. I pulled Mia's hair as I continued fucking her.

"Fucking christ, I am coming and I am coming now all over Papi's cock," she screamed saying.

Before I knew it, my cock throbbed and with a final thrust, I pumped all my huge load inside Mia's pussy.

Filling her up, and couldn't wait until she was all mine. As I pulled out of her pussy and despite, not wanting to.

My semen leaked out of Mia's cunt, which I scooped them all up with my fingers and pushed it more inside.

The last thing that I asked her. I hope that you can walk, as the night was far from over, and Mia laughed, saying;

"You wish, you could handle me, big boy."

And that night, I made her retrieve all her statements as Mia screamed all through the night as I fucked her so good.

CHAPTER FIFTEEN

ROMEO GIUSEPPE

As we stood in my room, wrapped in each other's arms, the city lights twinkled like distant stars outside the window, casting a soft glow that enveloped us. The steamy night had left us both breathless, yet it was this tranquil moment that spoke volumes—a silent testament to our undeniable connection.

 I ran my fingers gently through Mia's hair, relishing the way she leaned into my touch, her eyes fluttering closed in utter contentment. The intimacy of this moment wrapped around us like a cocoon, warm and safe, shielding us from the world outside.

"Bella, you make me feel alive," I whispered, my lips grazing her ear, every word infused with sincerity, a vow laced with the sweetness of the moment.

A soft smile graced her lips, and she sighed, the sound a melody of pure bliss. "You make me feel safe, Romeo."

Hearing those words ignited a fierce protectiveness within me, a primal urge to shield her from any harm. I pulled her closer, wrapping her in the warmth of my embrace, feeling her heartbeat against my chest.

"You are safe with me, always," I promised, my voice low and husky, a vow that resonated deeply in the quiet of the room.

The outside world faded into oblivion, leaving only the two of us lost in our private universe. In this sanctuary, my room, our love became the only truth that mattered. As I held Mia close, I felt an overwhelming sense of purpose swell within me: I would move heaven and earth to keep her safe and to keep her mine.

But a shadow loomed over our blissful moment. Thoughts of Jamie, her ex-boyfriend, crept into my mind, an unwelcome intruder that sent a chill through the warmth we had created. I was acutely aware of their complicated history, the lingering connection that still seemed to have a grip on her heart. That realization gnawed at me, a constant reminder of the battle I faced.

"Mia, can I ask you something?" I ventured gently, the weight of my curiosity pressing down on me.

"Of course, Romeo," she replied, her eyes still closed, an openness in her tone that gave me hope.

"What's going on with you and Jamie? I know you took a break from him, but I can tell he still affects you," I said, concern threading through my words, each syllable laden with the desire to understand.

Mia's eyes fluttered open, revealing a tumultuous mix of emotions—uncertainty, fear, and perhaps a flicker of hope.

"Romeo, I... I don't know. Jamie and I have a lot of history together. We were together for a long time, and it's hard to just cut ties completely," she confessed, her voice trembling slightly.

I nodded, trying to convey my understanding, even as a knot of worry twisted in my gut.

"I get that, bella. But I also know that he's not good for you. He's toxic, and he'll only hurt you again." My words came out with a fervor I couldn't suppress.

She sighed, the weight of my words sinking in like a stone.

"I know, Romeo. That's why I took a break from him. But it's hard to move on when you've invested so much of yourself in someone." Her voice broke slightly, revealing the vulnerability she carried within.

My heart ached for her, the intensity of my feelings crashing over me like a tidal wave. "You deserve so much better than him, Mia. You deserve someone who will love and respect you, someone who will make you happy. And I want to be that person."

Our eyes locked, and in that moment, I saw a glimmer of hope reflected in her gaze, a fragile yet beautiful thing.

"Romeo, I... I care about you deeply. But I need time to figure things out, to untangle my feelings." Her words hung in the air, heavy and bittersweet.

"Take all the time you need, bella. I'll be here, waiting for you," I reassured her, my voice steady, an anchor in the storm of emotions swirling between us.

Later that day, as I sat at my desk reviewing papers, my assistant buzzed in, interrupting my thoughts.

"Romeo, Jamie is here to see you." My eyebrows shot up, curiosity piqued at what he wanted, an uneasy tension tightening in my chest.

"Send him in," I instructed, bracing myself for the impending confrontation, my heart pounding in anticipation.

Jamie stormed into my office, his face twisted in anger, radiating hostility like a dark cloud.

"Stay away from Mia, Romeo," he growled, fists clenched at his sides, his body trembling with rage.

I leaned back in my chair, maintaining my calm despite the tempest brewing before me. "Jamie, what are you talking about?" I asked, my tone measured, laced with a sense of authority.

His face turned an alarming shade of red, the veins in his neck bulging.

"You know exactly what I'm talking about. You're trying to steal her away from me." His words dripped with venom, an accusation that cut deep.

I sighed, trying to reason with him, my patience wearing thin. "Jamie, Mia deserves better than you. She deserves someone who will love and respect her, not control and manipulate her."

For a fleeting moment, Jamie's face turned purple with rage, and I braced myself, expecting him to lunge at me. But he seemed to regain control, his anger simmering beneath the surface, a dangerous spark in his eyes.

"You'll never have her, Romeo. She'll always come back to me," he spat, the malice in his words unmistakable.

I stood, my eyes locked onto his, unwavering, a silent challenge between us. "Jamie, leave now. Before things get out of hand."

He snarled, his anger palpable, but I could see the hesitation creeping into his posture. For now, he backed down, but I knew this wouldn't be the last I'd see of him, a storm brewing on the horizon.

Later, I arrived at the Bianchi residence, my concern for Mia's safety weighing heavily on me after Jamie's threatening visit. As I entered the living room, I found Mr. Bianchi sitting on the couch, arms crossed, a stern expression etched on his face, like a sentinel guarding his fortress.

"Romeo, what are you doing here?" he asked gruffly, the tension palpable, every word dripping with caution.

"I need to speak with Mia, sir. Jamie's behavior is escalating, and I want to make sure she's safe. Plus, Evra would kill me if anything happened to her best friend," I explained, my voice firm yet respectful, every word a shield against the storm brewing between us.

Mr. Bianchi scowled, his gaze sharp as a blade. "You're not using your sister's friendship with Mia as an excuse to get close to her, Romeo. I know what you're capable of."

At that moment, Mia emerged from the hallway, worry etched on her face, a delicate flower caught in a tempest. "Dad, what's going on?"

Mr. Bianchi's expression turned even more stern. "Romeo here is concerned about your safety, Mia. But I've told him to stay away from you." His voice was resolute, a wall of protection he believed he was building around her.

Mia looked between us, confusion clouding her features. "But Romeo's always been nice to me, Dad. And Evra trusts him."

I could see the tension between them, a palpable current, and I knew Mr. Bianchi was hiding something, a truth buried beneath layers of concern. But I also understood the need to tread carefully, for Mia's sake and Evra's.

"I understand your concerns, Mr. Bianchi," I said, choosing my words carefully, each one a stepping stone in the delicate negotiation. "But I assure you, my intentions are pure. I only want to protect Mia from Jamie's toxic behavior."

Mr. Bianchi snorted, clearly unconvinced, his skepticism hanging in the air like a dense fog. "You think you're the only one who can protect her? I've been doing just fine without your help, Romeo."

I took a deep breath, determined not to escalate the situation further. "I'm not trying to undermine your authority, Mr. Bianchi. But as someone who cares about Mia, I want to help. And Evra would want me to help, too."

Mr. Bianchi's expression faltered for a moment, and I saw a flicker of understanding in his eyes, the gears turning as he processed my words. He realized that Evra and Mia were close and that Evra would want me to protect her friend.

"Fine," Mr. Bianchi said finally, the tension in the room easing slightly, though the air was still thick with unspoken warnings. "You can stay for now. But mark my words, Romeo: if you drag Mia into your world, you'll have to answer to me."

I nodded, relieved that the conversation hadn't escalated further. But I knew this was far from over. Mr. Bianchi would be watching me closely, and I had to tread carefully to avoid arousing his suspicions.

As I left the study, I saw Mia waiting for me in the living room, worry etched on her features, her eyes reflecting a mixture of trust and uncertainty. I knew I had to reassure her.

"Hey, bella," I said, trying to smile despite the lingering tension, my heart aching to ease her worries. "I'm here to protect you. I'll always be here."

She stepped closer, her gaze steady, and in that moment, I could see the resolve blossoming within her. "I know, Romeo. And I appreciate it. But I need to handle my battles too."

I nodded, understanding her need for independence, for strength in her own right. But my heart clenched with the knowledge that, no matter how strong she was, I would always be there, ready to fight alongside her in the shadows of our tangled lives.

CHAPTER SIXTEEN

ROMEO GIUSEPPE

I had everything planned—exposing Jamie's true nature, freeing Mia from his toxic grip, and finally making her mine. But life had other plans. Every day, I fought to maintain my distance, to give her the space she needed. But with each passing moment, my resolve crumbled. Every second without her felt like an eternity, an unsettling urgency gnawing at me. Time was slipping away.

Then came the cryptic message, summoning me to a secluded villa on the outskirts of town. The note offered little clarity, but one line burned in my mind: "Mia wants to see you." My heart raced. What did she want to reveal?

As I stepped into the villa, unease seeped into my bones. The lavish decor—marble columns, velvet sofas—felt cold and unwelcoming. And then I saw them: Jamie, Mia, and a handful of their closest friends. Jamie's smug expression twisted my gut, his fist clenched around a glinting ring, while Mia's wide eyes reflected shock and disbelief.

"Mia, from the moment I met you, I knew you were the one. Will you marry me?" His words dripped with insincerity. I watched as Mia's gaze darted around the room, desperately seeking an escape, but Jamie's grip on her hand was suffocating. She looked trapped, her spirit flickering like a dying flame.

"Say yes, Mia," Jamie's mother urged, her excitement jarring against the despair in the room. "You two are meant to be."

Mia's eyes met mine, and for a fleeting moment, I thought I saw hope. But then her gaze fell, shoulders slumping in resignation. "Yes," she whispered, her voice barely audible.

The room erupted in cheers, a cruel contrast to the horror boiling inside me. Jamie's family celebrated, while mine stood in stunned silence, the air thick with tension. It felt like a punch to the gut. Betrayal wrapped around my heart like a vice.

"Mia, don't do this," Evra whispered, her voice trembling. But Mia shook her head, her face etched with the weight of her decision.

"I've made up my mind," Mia said, her voice quivering with finality.

Jamie slid the ring onto her finger, his triumphant smile fueling the fire of my anger. "She said yes!" he crowed, his voice echoing like a funeral dirge.

I wanted to scream, to fight, but I felt paralyzed. How could Mia agree to marry him? Why was she sacrificing her happiness?

Evra confronted Mia, fury in her eyes. "How could you, Mia?" she spat. "You're marrying him? After everything?"

Mia lowered her gaze, her face pale. "Evra, please understand—"

"Understand?" Evra's laugh was bitter and raw. "You're throwing your happiness away for a man who doesn't love you. Jamie will suffocate you."

Jamie's face darkened. "That's enough, Evra," he growled, but Evra stood her ground.

"No, Jamie. You've fooled Mia, but you'll never fool us. We see through you."

Mia's voice broke the tension, barely a whisper. "I'm sorry, Evra. I know you don't approve, but I've made my choice."

Evra's expression shattered me. "Your choice? Mia, you're making a huge mistake."

I needed to stop this, to act, but I was frozen. I couldn't speak, couldn't move. I watched as Evra fled the room, her anger giving way to tears.

Mia's gaze flickered to mine, a faint spark of uncertainty in her eyes, but before I could say anything, Jamie's voice cut through the silence. "Well, that's settled then. Let's start planning the wedding."

Mia's shoulders sagged under the weight of her decision, and I turned and followed Evra out of the room, my heart heavy with sorrow.

In the hallway, Evra leaned against the wall, sobbing. I wrapped my arms around her, unable to comfort her fully. "She's making a mistake, Romeo," Evra whispered, her voice muffled against my chest.

"I know, Evra. I know."

Evra's anger flared again as she confronted Mia. "I begged you for one thing, Mia. Don't break my brother's heart. He loves you, and you chose him. Were you playing with his feelings?"

Mia's face crumpled, tears welling in her eyes. "Evra, please understand—"

"No, Mia! I don't want to understand!" Evra cried. "You knew how Romeo felt about you. You knew he loved you, and you still chose Jamie. You're breaking his heart, Mia. Don't you see that?"

Mia's mother shook her head, disappointment and anger etched across her face. "Mia, how could you be so foolish?"

Mia's father stood silently, his eyes fixed on Jamie, disgust in his gaze. He hated me, but the contempt for Jamie was far worse.

"I don't ever want to see you again, Mia," Evra spat, her voice trembling with rage. "You're dead to me. And as for you, Jamie, you'll pay for this one day."

With that, Evra turned and walked away, leaving Mia alone, her eyes cast down in defeat.

The room was silent, heavy with unspoken words. I watched Mia, standing there, a hollow shell of the woman I once knew.

The weight of my family's history had always cast a shadow over us, but I never thought it would drive her away. Jamie had offered her the stability I couldn't, and now, I questioned everything.

"I thought our love was enough," I whispered, the despair clear in my voice. "But was it ever enough for her?"

I stood there, frozen, lost in a storm of doubt. My love for Mia was real, but was it enough to fight against the safety that Jamie offered?

The room was empty now, the echoes of celebration fading into painful silence. I looked at Mia, standing alone, her back turned to me. In that moment, I realized we were both lost, trapped by fear and expectations.

"Why, Mia?" I finally asked, my voice thick with emotion. "Why him? After everything we've been through?"

She turned slowly, tears shimmering in her eyes. "I thought it was what I was supposed to do," she whispered. "I thought I could make it work. That maybe I could love him enough to forget..."

"Forget what?" I asked urgently. "Forget us? We had something real. Why are you throwing it away?"

"I know!" she cried, frustration and sorrow in her voice. "But Jamie offers stability. I thought I could be happy with him, but I didn't realize how much I was sacrificing."

"You're sacrificing yourself for a lie," I said softly. "You deserve more than what he can give you."

Her gaze wavered as the battle raged within her. "And what do you want me to do, Romeo? Walk away from everything? From the life I thought I wanted?"

"Walk away from the lie," I implored. "Choose love, not comfort. You deserve true happiness, with or without me."

She sobbed, her tears breaking me. "I don't know if I can," she whispered. "I'm scared."

"Scared of what?" I asked, my voice full of tenderness. "Of taking a chance? Of losing the safety he offers? Because I won't let you go, Mia. Not like this."

She looked up at me, her vulnerability raw. "What if I can't choose you?"

"Then I'll fight for you," I vowed, my resolve solidifying. "I'll fight for your happiness, for your heart."

Mia hesitated, torn between what she thought she wanted and the love she deserved. I knew we were at a crossroads, a decision that would change everything.

"Just think about it," I urged, stepping back, giving her space. "You don't have to decide now. But know this: my love for you is real. And I'll always be here, waiting for you to choose the right path."

As I turned to leave, I glanced back one last time. Mia stood motionless, her eyes filled with turmoil. A tiny spark of hope flickered in my chest. Maybe, just maybe, she would find the courage to choose the path back to me.

CHAPTER SEVENTEEN

MIA BIANCHI

My heart raced as I stared at Jamie's message on my phone: "Meet me at the old oak tree at 5 PM. Come alone." A sense of dread washed over me, icy waves crashing onto the shore of my sanity. It was as if I were trapped in a recurring nightmare, I thought I had finally escaped.

Memories of our toxic relationship flooded my mind—the way Jamie would guilt-trip me, twisting my words and manipulating my emotions to get what he wanted. Months had passed since our breakup, yet he still wouldn't let me go. His messages, constant calls, and unexpected visits were persistent reminders that I wasn't free. Each notification felt like a chain clanking around my heart, binding me to a past I desperately wanted to leave behind.

I shook the thoughts from my head, but the unease gnawed at me as I drove to the old oak tree. Arriving, the air felt thick with anticipation, the weight of my decision pressing down on my chest. The towering tree loomed over me, its gnarled branches casting long shadows across the ground, like dark fingers reaching for me.

Jamie was already there, standing under the tree, his figure a stark silhouette against the fading sunlight. His eyes locked onto mine with an unnerving intensity, sending a chill racing down my spine as he stepped forward.

"Mia, I've missed you so much," he said, his voice smooth, almost too smooth. There was a heaviness in the way he said my name, as though it carried the weight of unspoken expectations. "I can't live without you. If you don't come back to me, I'll... I'll hurt myself. I'll make sure you regret leaving me."

The words hit me like a punch to the stomach. Guilt surged through me, mingled with fear. I knew Jamie was capable of hurting himself, and the thought twisted my insides into knots. A part of me wanted to reach out, to comfort him, but I knew I couldn't. I couldn't let myself fall into his manipulations again.

"Jamie, please don't say that," I whispered, my voice trembling. "Let's talk about this calmly." My heart ached, longing for the man I once loved, buried deep beneath the hurt and anger.

But Jamie shook his head, his eyes hardening with resolve. "No, Mia. I need you to promise me you'll marry me. If you don't, I'll expose your secrets. I'll ruin your reputation, destroy your relationships. You'll be all alone."

His words felt like a tightening noose, the pressure building, suffocating me. My thoughts scrambled, fighting between the need to protect myself and the fear of what he might do next. I couldn't let my past be exposed. I had no choice but to comply, or risk losing everything.

The scene shifted around me as I found myself inside a grand hall later that evening. The crowd was a blur of faces, their laughter and chatter a stark contrast to the turmoil raging inside me. The clink of glasses and the smell of fine food filled the air, but I could barely focus on anything but the weight of Jamie's arm around me. I felt like I was drowning in a sea of expectations, playing a role I never wanted.

Jamie's mother led me to the center of the room, her smile wide and proud as she presented me to the gathering. I caught Romeo's gaze from across the room. His eyes, full of concern and understanding, sent a ripple of guilt through me. I wanted to reach out to him, but the weight of Jamie's grip on my arm kept me tethered to this charade.

The room fell silent as Jamie raised his glass, his voice booming with false cheer. "Ladies and gentlemen, family and friends, I present to you my fiancée, Mia!"

Applause erupted around us, but all I felt was suffocating pressure. Jamie's words echoed in my mind, drowning out everything else. Guilt, regret, and the overwhelming sense of being trapped flooded me. I knew this wasn't what I wanted, but I couldn't find the strength to say no—not in front of all these people.

I glanced around the room, my eyes desperately searching for a sign, for someone to rescue me from this nightmare. But all I saw were faces full of expectation, their smiles too wide, too eager. I couldn't escape.

"Yes... Yes, I'll marry you, Jamie," I finally whispered, the words barely audible but enough to break me.

The moment the words left my lips, a wave of relief washed over me—but it was quickly replaced by a crushing sense of guilt and anxiety. I'd made a mistake, but there was no taking it back now. The applause that followed felt deafening, like the sound of chains tightening around me.

Jamie's family erupted into cheers, their faces full of joy and approval, but there was no joy in me. Only a hollow emptiness. Across the room, Evra's eyes blazed with anger and disappointment, and I felt the weight of her gaze like a slap to the face.

"Mia, how could you?" she shouted, her voice cutting through the air, sharp and accusing. The sound of her anger filled the room, and I shrank under the pressure.

Jamie's fingers dug into my arm, his grip tightening as he leaned in close.

"Smile, Mia," he hissed, his voice dark and commanding. "We're happy, aren't we?" The threat behind his words sent a shiver down my spine.

I forced a smile, but it felt like a mask. Inside, I was screaming. I was drowning. The applause still echoed in my ears, but it felt like a funeral dirge. Had I just made the worst mistake of my life?

"I knew you'd see it my way, Mia," Jamie whispered, his voice dripping with smug satisfaction.

Regret and anger bubbled up inside me, but it was too late. I was caught in this toxic cycle, and the worst part was, I didn't know how to break free. Every passing moment felt like a countdown to something worse.

As the night wore on, I went through the motions, smiling and nodding as Jamie's family congratulated us. But with every passing moment, the weight of my decision grew heavier. I locked eyes with Romeo once more, and his expression mirrored mine—deep sadness and a quiet understanding. He knew. He knew I was trapped, and there was nothing he could do.

When the night finally ended, Jamie's grip on my hand was unrelenting, possessive. "You're mine now, Mia," he whispered, his voice cold with ownership.

A chill ran down my spine as a dark cloud of dread settled over me. I had to find a way out. I had to find the strength to leave this toxic relationship before it consumed me completely. But for now, I was trapped, playing the role of the happy fiancée. And I didn't know how much longer I could pretend.

CHAPTER EIGHTEEN

ROMEO GIUSEPPE

I feel like I've been gutted—my insides ripped out and left to bleed on the floor. Every breath is a struggle as the scene replays in my mind, an endless loop of Mia's radiant smile lighting up the room, Jamie's triumphant grin shining like a beacon, and the applause still echoing in my ears. It's a haunting melody I can't shake, surreal yet painfully real—a visceral reminder of the heartache that consumes me.

"Why did she do it? Why did she choose him over me?" The questions claw at me, relentless and unforgiving. I thought what we had was stronger than this—woven from shared moments and whispered dreams. But perhaps I was mistaken. Perhaps I was always wrong, forever destined to misinterpret the signs.

"Perché, Mia, perché?" I whisper, my voice cracking under the weight of my emotions, each syllable heavy with despair. "Why, Mia, why?"

I shake my head, desperately trying to clear the fog clouding my thoughts, but I can't. The truth looms before me, painful and undeniable. I was a fool, blinded by hope and love that now feels like a cruel joke.

Deep down, I knew she wasn't over him. I knew she was still trapped in that toxic cycle, spinning endlessly in his web of manipulation and deceit. But I thought... I thought my love could be enough to break her free, to shatter the chains that bound her. I believed in us, in the promise of a future filled with love and laughter.

"Sono stato così stupido," I mutter, tears welling in my eyes, blurring my vision like rain on a foggy window. "I was so stupid."

From the next room, I hear my parents speaking in hushed tones, their worry palpable, especially now. I strain to listen, catching snippets of the conversation between Mr. and Mrs. Bianchi and my parents, their voices laced with concern.

"Mrs. Bianchi, wait," my father says, his voice low but urgent, a hint of desperation seeping through. "We need to talk about Romeo."

"Di cosa si tratta?" Mrs. Bianchi's voice trembles with concern, a mother's instinct to protect her child evident in her tone. "What's wrong?"

"We're worried about him," my mother replies softly, her voice cracking like fragile glass. "He's not healing. He's just... existing. We're afraid of losing him to his pain."

"Abbiamo paura di perderlo," my father adds, his voice trembling with fear. "We're afraid of losing him."

As the door closes behind Mrs. Bianchi, I hear my parents' voices drop even further, their concern intensifying, wrapping around me like a heavy blanket.

"Dobbiamo essere pazienti," my mother insists, her words a soothing balm laced with sadness, as if she's trying to soothe a wound that won't heal. "We need to be patient."

"Sì, ma per quanto tempo?" My father's frustration spills over, his voice rising slightly, the raw emotion evident. "Yes, but for how long?"

I lie still in bed, trying to keep quiet, but their words cut deep, piercing through the fog of my thoughts like a knife. Guilt coils inside me, a heavy weight I can't shake off. I hate that they have to go through this because of me, this silent suffering that wraps around our family like a shroud.

"Mi dispiace, Mamma, Papà," I whisper to myself, a futile apology escaping my lips, echoing in the emptiness of the room. "I'm sorry, Mom, Dad."

But no amount of apologies will change what's happened. Mia didn't love me—not truly. She didn't care enough to fight for us. Mrs. Bianchi's words echo in my mind, a constant reminder of the truth I had been too blind to see.

She only liked me. She never loved me.

The realization sinks its claws into my heart, ripping it apart with a merciless grip. Fresh tears well up, but I choke them back, unwilling to succumb to the grief that threatens to swallow me whole.

"Non mi ama," I whisper, the words tasting bitter and toxic, as if they're laced with poison. "She doesn't love me. È solo interessata a lui, sempre lui." She's only ever interested in him, always him.

I want to shove these thoughts away, but they cling to me like shadows, lurking and festering, a relentless reminder of my failures. And neither can my parents escape their worry for me.

I hear it in their voices—how scared they are that I'll break beyond repair. It's as if they're waiting for me to collapse under the weight of it all, to crumble into a million pieces they'll never be able to pick up. Their concern is a living thing, breathing life into the fears that already gnaw at me.

"Sono preoccupati per me," I think, the truth striking me like a blow to the chest. They're worried about me. "E hanno ragione di esserlo." And they're right to be.

The silence that follows is stifling, thick with everything left unsaid. I can feel their fear seeping through the walls, amplifying my own, creating a suffocating atmosphere that leaves me gasping for breath.

I want to tell them I'll be okay, that I'm strong enough to pull through this. But I can't. I don't know how to reassure them when I don't even believe it myself, the words dying on my lips.

"Sono perso," I whisper, feeling my chest tighten with the weight of despair that feels like a leaden anchor dragging me down. "I'm lost. Non so come uscire da questo buio." I don't know how to escape this darkness that wraps around me, suffocating and unyielding.

I lie there, trapped in my thoughts, the silence stretching on endlessly. The longer it goes, the deeper I fall, like a stone sinking into a bottomless abyss. I'm sinking into something I don't know how to get out of, each moment pulling me further into despair.

"Ci riuscirò mai a uscire da questo dolore?" Will I ever be able to escape this pain? The question echoes in my mind like a cruel taunt, reverberating in the empty chambers of my heart. Will I always be haunted by her memory? By the emptiness she left behind? The uncertainty gnaws at me, and the only thing I'm sure of is that I'm trapped.

"E tutto quello che so," I murmur, the weight of my reality crashing down around me like a tidal wave. "And that's all I know. Sono intrappolato in questo dolore, e non so come uscire." I'm trapped in this pain, and I don't know how to escape.

I stare up at the ceiling, waiting for something—anything— that might offer a glimmer of hope. But all I see is darkness, an unyielding void that swallows everything in its path.

"Aspetto una luce nella oscurità," I whisper, my voice trembling with vulnerability, a soft prayer to the universe. "I wait for a light in the darkness. Una luce che mi guidi verso la guarigione." A light that will guide me toward healing, toward redemption, away from this suffocating anguish.

But until that day comes, until I find that light, I'm stuck here—in this limbo, unable to move forward, unable to let go of the pain that chains me to my despair.

"Sono intrappolato," I whisper, my voice cracking with raw emotion, the weight of my sorrow threatening to crush me. "I'm trapped. E non so come uscire." And I don't know how to escape.

CHAPTER NINETEEN

ROMEO GIUSEPPE

I stood in front of the mirror, staring at the stranger reflected in me. My eyes, once bright with hope, now appeared sharp and hollow, the shadows beneath them hinting at the sleepless nights spent wrestling with my thoughts.

Weeks of isolation had stripped me down to someone I barely recognized—a man hardened by betrayal and driven by a growing hunger for power. The reflection was a ghost of the boy I used to be, now replaced by a figure consumed by the darkness that was slowly overtaking my soul.

"Romeo, il giovane capo," my father's voice echoed in my head, a lingering reminder of the weight of expectation. "You are the future of our family." His words clung to me like chains, pulling me deeper into the shadows I was beginning to embrace. I could almost feel the darkness crawling up my spine, wrapping around my thoughts like a shroud, whispering promises of vengeance.

The dim light flickered, as if sensing the shift within me, casting unsettling shadows on the walls that mirrored the turmoil inside my chest.

I paced the room, my footsteps echoing, my mind racing with thoughts of revenge and power. Mia's face flashed in my memory—her radiant smile, the warmth of her laughter, the sparkle in her eyes—now twisted by painful memories of her tears, her fear.

How could I have been so blind? So weak to let her slip away, to let her become a victim of Jamie's cruelty?

The door creaked open behind me, and Luca stood there, his posture tight with tension.

"Capo, we have a problem," he said, his voice steady, but the urgency in his eyes spoke volumes.

"What is it?" I snapped, irritation leaking through. My mind was already tangled in dark thoughts, and I didn't want distractions.

"The rival families are circling like vultures. They think we're weak."

A cold smile spread across my face as I turned to face him, the thrill of impending chaos sparking a fire in my chest.

"Then we'll show them just how wrong they are. Let them come. They'll find out that we're anything but weak."

Luca nodded, but before I could issue further orders, the door burst open again. Mia stumbled in, and my heart stopped. Her face was bruised, her lip split, blood staining the collar of her shirt, twisting my stomach into knots of rage and despair.

"Mia! Dio mio, what happened to you?" I crossed the room in an instant, my hands hovering over her as she collapsed into a chair, trembling with pain and fear.

She tried to speak, but her voice choked on sobs that shredded my heart. "Romeo... I didn't know where else to go. He... he..."

"Who did this?" My voice shook with barely contained fury, but when her tear-filled eyes met mine, I swallowed the fire threatening to erupt. I knelt in front of her, my hands gently cupping her bruised face, feeling the heat of her skin.

"Mia, who did this?" I implored, desperation thick in my voice.

Her lip trembled, tears spilling down her cheeks. "Jamie... after the engagement party... He was drunk. He said things. Did things... I was so scared."

My fists clenched, nails biting into my palms, fury coursing through my veins like poison. Jamie would pay for this—he would suffer for every tear she'd shed, for every bruise on her beautiful skin.

"I have to leave, Romeo," she whispered, her voice breaking as she looked at me with wide, frightened eyes. "But I don't know where to go."

The weight of her words hit me like a freight train. I nodded, my mind already spinning with plans, but before she could leave, I raised my phone, the camera flash lighting the room as I captured images of her injuries.

"Evidence," I said, my voice cold, almost clinical.

She flinched but nodded, the strength draining from her as she seemed to fade into the night, leaving me with one burning thought: Jamie would regret ever laying a hand on her.

"Luca!" I barked, my voice sharp and commanding.

He appeared instantly, his face hard, ready for whatever I needed.

"Capo?"

"We need everything on Jamie. His associates, his family, his weaknesses—I want to know what he eats for breakfast."

Luca's lips curled into a grim smile, a look that promised retribution.

"Understood, capo."

As he left, I stood by the window, staring into the night. The air outside was thick with tension, mirroring the storm that raged within me. I could feel the weight of my decision pressing down on me like a boulder, knowing there would be no turning back.

But one thing was certain—Jamie would pay. I would not stop until I destroyed everything he ever loved, and I would relish every moment of it.

CHAPTER TWENTY

MIA BIANCHI

After leaving Romeo's office, I knew I had to hide. Jamie would stop at nothing to find me, and the thought sent icy tendrils of fear snaking down my spine. I made my way to a small café on the outskirts of town—a cozy, unassuming spot I hoped would help me blend into the background. The comforting aroma of freshly brewed coffee wrapped around me like a warm embrace as I stepped inside, ordering my drink and settling into a quiet corner. My heart raced with anxiety.

As I sat there, trying to collect my scattered thoughts, my gaze drifted to the door. That's when I spotted him—Romeo. His commanding presence filled the room, his tall frame exuding confidence as his eyes swept the café, searching. A smile tugged at my lips, knowing I was safely hidden behind my disguise. My breath hitched with the adrenaline that surged through me.

"Caffè Italiano. Come find me," I quickly typed and sent the text, my heart pounding with anticipation.

Romeo's expression softened as he read my message, and his eyes finally found mine. He made his way toward me with a purposeful stride, a warm smile spreading across his face. "Mia, amore," he whispered as he slid into the seat beside me, his eyes sparkling with relief. "You look beautiful in that disguise."

Heat flooded my cheeks, and a flutter stirred in my stomach. "Grazie, Romeo. I just wanted to be safe."

His fingers found mine, intertwining gently, his eyes never leaving mine with an intensity that promised protection. "You're always safe with me, Mia. I promise."

Just then, the door creaked open with a jarring sound that sent a chill rushing down my spine. Jamie stepped inside, his presence instantly darkening the atmosphere. My heart dropped as his eyes began scanning the room, and a surge of fear washed over me. But Romeo's grip on my hand tightened, grounding me. "Don't worry, Mia. I've got you," he murmured, his voice steady but low.

Jamie's gaze landed on us, his face contorting into a mask of rage as he stormed over, fists clenched. "Mia, you're a cheat!" he spat, his voice echoing through the café like a shot. "You're a slut, just like your mother!"

The words hit me like a slap, and Romeo's hand tightened further, his jaw clenching in a fierce display of control. "Jamie, calm down," he warned, his voice cold and authoritative. "This isn't the place for this."

But Jamie wouldn't listen. His face twisted into a sneer. "You think you're so much better than us, Romeo?" he hissed, contempt dripping from his words. "You're just a dirty Italian bastard!"

For a moment, I thought Romeo would lash out, but instead, he held himself back, his face twisting with disgust. "I won't stoop to your level, Jamie," he said, rising from his seat with a grace that betrayed the tension in his posture. "Mia, let's go."

I hesitated, torn between fear and loyalty, my heart aching at the thought of leaving Romeo alone to face Jamie's fury. His eyes locked onto mine, intensity and urgency radiating from them. "Please, Mia," he whispered, desperation lacing his words. "I don't want you to see me like this."

Before I could respond, Romeo turned and walked away, leaving me alone with Jamie's rage. Jamie's expression twisted into something darker, and he reached for me, his grip like iron on my arm, sending pain shooting up my skin.

"You're a narcissistic bitch, Mia!" he snarled, his voice ringing harshly in my ears. "You think you're perfect with your mixed blood and fake smile?"

"Let me go, Jamie!" I shouted, struggling to break free, but he only laughed—a sound that froze my blood in my veins. "You're a slut, Mia. A dirty, half-breed whore. You're nothing but trash!"

His words struck deep, but I fought to hold back tears, thrashing against his unyielding grip as he dragged me out of the café. The faces of the other patrons blurred in my peripheral vision—expressions of shock and pity—as Jamie's anger consumed my reality. He shoved me into his car, slamming the door shut with a force that made my chest tighten. I was trapped.

As Jamie slid into the driver's seat, his eyes burned with fury, igniting a fire of dread deep in my gut. "You're going to pay for what you did, Mia," he growled, each word dripping with venom. "You're going to pay for leaving me."

I shrank into the corner of the car, my heart pounding as I looked out the window, desperately hoping for a sign of Romeo. Where was he? Why hadn't he come back for me?

The engine roared to life, and we sped away, leaving the café and my dwindling hope behind. The atmosphere shifted as Jamie opened the door to his house, the familiar creak of the hinges echoing through the dimly lit hallway. The air inside felt thick, suffocating, as if the house itself were holding its breath, waiting for the storm to break.

"Jamie, I think we need to talk about—" I began, but before I could finish, his face contorted in violent rage. His hand moved faster than I could react, and the sharp crack of the slap shattered the silence, sending me stumbling backward. My hand shot to my throbbing cheek.

"What the hell, Jamie?" I gasped, my voice trembling with shock and pain. But he didn't answer. His eyes—once warm and inviting—were now cold, unrecognizable, filled with a darkness I had never seen before.

Without warning, he lunged again, fists clenched. He struck me with a sickening force, and I raised my arms to shield myself, but the blows kept coming. The room around us began to blur as pain consumed me, my vision swimming. I tasted blood, its metallic tang spreading across my mouth, trickling down my chin. The world around me spun, the edges softening into a haze.

I could feel my strength draining, and I crumpled to the floor, the cold tiles pressing against my bruised skin. "Please... stop..." I whimpered, my voice barely a whisper as darkness began to creep into the corners of my vision.

Jamie stood over me, chest heaving, but his face showed no remorse—only cold, indifferent rage. The room fell into eerie silence, save for the sound of my shallow breaths.

With one final, trembling gasp, I slipped into unconsciousness.

The house seemed to hold its breath, the only sound the faint drip of blood pooling on the floor. Jamie stood over my motionless body, his breath ragged. The weight of his actions began to settle into the quiet stillness. His rage, mixed with betrayal, pulsed through him as he screamed, "You're just pretending, you cheating ass!" His voice oozed with venom. "You think you can just fake it, and I'll stop?"

But I didn't move. My body remained still, limp, pale, and unresponsive. Jamie's blows slowed, his breathing heavy as he stared at me, waiting for any sign of life, any reaction. But I gave none.

A creeping panic settled in his chest. He knelt beside me, trembling hands reaching for my pulse. It was weak, faint.

"No, no, no," Jamie muttered, his voice cracking with panic. "You can't be... You're just pretending."

But deep down, he knew. He had gone too far.

With a snarl, Jamie stood, his eyes blazing with a toxic mixture of anger and fear. "You're not worth it," he spat, turning away from my still form. "You're nothing but a cheating, lying, worthless..." His words trailed off as he stormed out of the house, leaving me to die in the suffocating silence.

CHAPTER TWENTY-ONE

ROMEO GIUSEPPE

I couldn't shake the growing unease that had settled in since Mia left the café. A knot twisted in my stomach, the sensation crawling beneath my skin, prickling with urgency. It was an instinct born of familiarity—something was dreadfully wrong. Without hesitation, I called in a favor from Emilio, a loyalty forged in the fires of our shared past. He owed me, and now was the time to collect.

"Keep an eye on her," I instructed, my voice tight with a mixture of worry and determination, each word tinged with the weight of my fear. "I need to know everything."

Emilio nodded, his face serious, and disappeared into the shadows, leaving me in a state of restless anticipation. Time stretched on, each second feeding the gnawing anxiety inside me like a relentless predator. When Emilio returned, his expression was dark, and my heart sank like a stone.

"Romeo, we've got a problem," he said, his voice barely above a whisper, laden with dread. "Jamie left the house in a panic... Mia isn't moving."

The words hit me like a punch to the gut, a visceral panic gripping me. "What do you mean she's not moving?" I demanded, fear tightening my chest like a vise.

"She's just lying there, man. I didn't see her breathing."

Adrenaline surged through me like wildfire, igniting every nerve ending in my body. There was no time to think, only to act. "Give me the address," I barked, my heart pounding, each beat a desperate plea for Mia's safety.

Emilio hesitated for just a moment, and in that silence, I could feel the weight of impending disaster. He handed me a scrap of paper, its corners crumpled from anxiety, and without wasting another second, I bolted out of there, my feet pounding against the pavement, praying I wasn't too late.

When I arrived, the house loomed before me, dark and foreboding, eerily quiet as if it held its breath, anticipating what was about to unfold. I knocked, my fist striking the door with urgency, but there was no answer. My pulse roared in my ears like a thunderous drum. With a surge of determination, I kicked open the door, the wood splintering under the force of my desperation.

Then I saw her.

Mia.

Lying lifeless on the floor.

"Mia, amore mio," I whispered, a choked sob escaping my lips as I rushed to her side, panic rising like a tide inside me. I knelt beside her, my trembling hands checking for a pulse, every second stretching into eternity.

It was faint, but it was there. Thank God.
Scooping her up, her body felt alarmingly limp in my arms, as if all the warmth had been drained from her. "Hang on, Mia.

Please, hang on," I begged, my voice breaking as I grabbed my phone to call for help. The operator's calm voice tried to guide me through the chaos, but my thoughts spiraled out of control, a chaotic whirlwind of fear and urgency. "Mia, stay with me. Dio mio, stay with me," I whispered in Italian, my voice trembling as I cradled her closer, feeling the cold weight of dread settle in my chest while I waited for the ambulance. Each passing second felt like an eternity, time stretching in a cruel mockery of my desperation.

Finally, the sirens wailed in the distance, a promise of hope racing toward us. The paramedics arrived, moving with the efficiency of trained professionals. "Per favore, fate presto!" I urged them, my heart pounding in sync with the chaos around us.

I watched helplessly as they worked to stabilize her, their movements precise but filled with an urgency that sent ice through my veins. The rhythmic beeping of machines filled the air, each sound a reminder of how precarious her situation was.

I couldn't breathe until we were in the ambulance, rushing toward the hospital, the fluorescent lights overhead flickering ominously, casting harsh shadows across Mia's pale face. Each passing moment felt like a countdown, a race against time where the stakes were her life.

At the hospital, the waiting room felt suffocating, every tick of the clock echoing in the heavy silence like a death knell. Our families arrived, their faces etched with worry, the atmosphere thick with unspoken fears and tension. My sister, Evra, approached me, her eyes filled with tears that threatened to spill over.

"Romeo, I'm so sorry," she whispered, her voice trembling with the weight of her guilt. "I didn't know Jamie would do this."
"Non importa," I muttered, shaking my head, dismissing her blame. "It's not your fault. I will make sure he never gets near her again."

The wait dragged on, each minute heavier than the last, a torturous reminder of the uncertainty looming over us. Finally, the doctor let me see Mia.

I stepped into the room, my heart in my throat, dread clawing at my insides. She looked so fragile lying there, her bruises stark against her pale skin, a heartbreaking testament to the violence she'd endured. It shattered something deep within me, the sight of her vulnerable and broken.

"Mia," I whispered, taking her hand, which felt cold and unresponsive. "Why didn't you leave him?"

Her eyes fluttered open, a weak smile tugging at her lips, a flicker of life amidst the pain. "I was scared," she whispered, her voice barely audible, as if speaking too loudly might shatter the fragile moment.

I squeezed her hand, guilt clawing at my insides like a ravenous beast. "I should've been there for you," I whispered in Italian, my voice breaking. "Sarei dovuto essere lì per te."

Her eyes locked onto mine, a flicker of hope glimmering in their depths. "You're here now," she whispered, her voice faint but sure. "That's all that matters."

Just then, Mia's mother stormed into the room, her face twisted with a mix of anger and fear, her presence a whirlwind of emotion. "Mia, how could you go back to him?" she demanded, her voice sharp and accusatory, each word a dagger aimed at Mia's heart. "After everything he's done to you?"

I stepped forward, trying to calm her, to bridge the gap between fury and understanding. "Signora, this isn't Mia's fault. Jamie's actions—"

She cut me off, her eyes blazing with a mother's fury. "She should have trusted you, Romeo. If only she had stayed away from him, none of this would've happened."

Mia flinched, her eyes filled with guilt as she shrank into herself, as if the weight of her mother's words was too much to bear. "Mamma, I was scared... I didn't know what else to do."

Her mother's expression softened, the fire in her gaze dimming, but her voice remained stern, filled with the authority of a parent who had witnessed too much pain.

"You should have trusted Romeo. He's the only one who's always cared for you."

I nodded, my heart aching for Mia, for the struggle she had faced alone, lost in a whirlwind of confusion and fear. "We'll get through this together," I whispered, holding her hand tightly, my resolve unyielding.

Mia broke down, her sobs wracking her fragile body, a heartbreaking release of fear and regret. "I'm sorry... I was so blind."

I pulled her close, pressing a gentle kiss to her forehead, the warmth of my breath a soft comfort against the chill that lingered in the room. "Shh, amore mio. We'll get through this. Together."

As Mia's tears slowed, her mother sighed and stepped back, the weight of the moment settling over us like a shroud, a delicate pause in the storm of emotions swirling around us. "Just promise me, Mia... never again. Trust Romeo. Trust yourself."

Mia nodded weakly, her voice hoarse from crying, each word a fragile promise. "I promise."

The room fell silent, the weight of everything sinking in like an anchor in deep water. Our families filed out, leaving us alone in the quiet, the sterile smell of antiseptic filling the air. I sat beside Mia, my hand gently stroking her hair, the rhythm of her breathing becoming my only solace amidst the chaos that had consumed our lives.

The journey ahead would be long and fraught with challenges, but I would be with her every step of the way. "I'll never let him hurt you again, Mia," I whispered, a promise sealed with the deepest part of my soul, vowing to shield her from the darkness that had almost claimed her.

CHAPTER TWENTY-TWO

MIA BIANCHI

I slowly opened my eyes, greeted by the familiar sight of the sterile white ceiling above me, its unforgiving brightness competing with the dull ache thumping relentlessly in my head. I let out a soft groan, the sound barely piercing the thick fog of confusion clouding my mind.

How long had I been confined to this bed? Days? Weeks? Perhaps months? Time blurred together in an endless cycle of pain and monotony, each moment stretching and contracting like the rhythm of my labored breaths.
As I turned my head slightly, the door creaked open, and Dr. Lee entered the room, his expression grim, casting a shadow over the fragile flicker of hope that dared to ignite within me. I could see the weight of concern etched across his features, his brow furrowed, and his eyes heavy with the burden of bad news.

"Mia," he began, his voice steady yet laced with an undercurrent of urgency, "we've got some concerns about your internal injuries."

He paused, allowing the gravity of his words to sink in. "The scans show a ruptured spleen and possible damage to your liver."

Panic surged through me, a tidal wave crashing against the fragile shoreline of my composure. My eyes widened in alarm, desperation clawing at my throat. "What does that mean?" I asked, my voice trembling as dread coiled tightly in my stomach.

Dr. Lee hesitated, his gaze drifting to the floor as he weighed his words carefully, as if each one carried the weight of my fate. "It means we need to monitor you closely for signs of further complications. We may need to perform surgery to repair the damage."

As if on cue, Romeo's grip on my hand tightened, his fingers intertwining with mine, radiating warmth and urgency. "Che cosa significa?" (What does it mean?) he demanded, his voice thick with concern, eyes searching Dr. Lee's face for answers.

Dr. Lee explained the risks in a calm yet somber tone, detailing the potential outcomes with a clarity that felt both clinical and terrifying. I could see the color drain from Romeo's face, the weight of the news settling upon him like a shroud. It was as if the air had grown thick with uncertainty, choking us both.

"Dio mio," (My God) he whispered, turning to me, anguish flickering in his eyes like a candle threatened by the winds of fate. "Amore mio, I'm so sorry. I feel helpless." His voice cracked, each syllable a jagged piece of glass that cut through the silence.
My heart ached at the sight of his pain. "I just want to go home, Romeo. I want to be free from this pain." The words spilled from my lips, raw and unfiltered, heavy with longing.

Romeo's face softened, determination mingling with sorrow in his gaze. "Lo so, amore mio," (I know, my love) he whispered, the promise in his voice wrapping around me like a protective embrace. "But please, just a little longer. We'll get through this together, insieme." The final word lingered in the air, a shared vow that transcended the darkness surrounding us.

Days dragged on, stretching like taffy in a hot sun, my frustration growing into a relentless tide washing over me. I was trapped in this endless cycle of pain and medication, unable to escape the confines of my own body.

Though Romeo's presence remained a constant comfort, a beacon in my shadowed world, even his unwavering love couldn't chase away the darkness that loomed overhead.

One afternoon, desperation reached a boiling point, a fire igniting within me. I turned to him, my eyes blazing with an unquenchable need for freedom. "I need to get out of here, Romeo. I need to feel alive again." My voice was a fierce whisper, a challenge hurled against the oppressive weight of my circumstances.

His expression transformed, fierce determination flooding his features. "Sì, amore mio," (Yes, my love) he said, his voice firm yet tender, resonating with the promise of a shared battle. "We'll get through this together. Andrà tutto bene." (Everything will be alright.)

Though his words soothed the storm within me, I still felt trapped, like a bird in a gilded cage. "Romeo, I need to get out of here," I insisted, my voice resolute and unwavering.

"I need to feel the sun on my skin, the wind in my hair, to know that I'm still alive!" The last word came out almost as a plea, echoing against the sterile walls.

His gaze softened, filled with understanding and concern that swirled within his deep brown eyes. "Amore mio, I understand. But we can't risk it yet. Jamie's still out there, and I won't put you in danger." The finality in his voice struck a chord within me, a painful reminder of the shadows lurking outside these walls.

"Non posso perderti, Mia," (I can't lose you, Mia) he whispered, his voice trembling with the weight of his emotions, his grip tightening around my hand like a lifeline.

My frustration boiled over, a hot wave of defiance coursing through my veins. "I don't care about Jamie! I care about living my life!"

The words burst forth, fueled by a primal instinct to reclaim my existence. Romeo's grip tightened further, a silent vow echoing in his touch, a promise I desperately clung to.

"I know, Mia. And I'll do everything to make sure you can live your life, free from fear. But please, just a little longer." "Solo un po' più di tempo, amore mio," (Just a little more time, my love) he murmured, his voice softening as he gazed into my eyes, searching for the resolve to believe in this shared future.

As days turned into weeks, my body slowly began to heal, but my spirit remained shackled, longing for freedom and normalcy. One day, as the golden rays of the sun filtered through the window, illuminating the dull room, Romeo entered with surprise, his face a beacon of hope.

"Amore mio, I have a gift for you," he said, holding up a small, delicate flower—a vibrant bloom of color amidst the clinical surroundings. "Ecco, una piccola cosa per te." (Here, a small thing for you.)

My eyes widened in delight, the flower's radiance captivating against the sterile backdrop of the hospital. "Oh, Romeo! It's beautiful!" I exclaimed, a smile breaking through the shadows of my despair.

He smiled back, warmth radiating from him like the sun itself. "I thought it would bring some joy to your day. And maybe, just maybe, it will remind you that there's still beauty in the world, even in the darkest times." His gaze held mine, the connection between us palpable. "La bellezza è sempre lì, amore mio, anche nei momenti più bui." (Beauty is always there, my love, even in the darkest moments.)

The day of the surgery arrived, anxiety coiling tightly in my chest, a serpent ready to strike. Romeo held my hand, his eyes locked onto mine, a lifeline amidst the chaos. "Tutto andrà bene, amore mio," (Everything will be alright, my love) he whispered, his voice a soothing balm against my fears, grounding me in the moment.

Dr. Lee entered the room, his face serious, yet his demeanor radiating professionalism. "Mia, are you ready?" he asked, his voice steady.

I nodded, my heart racing with anticipation, a mix of fear and determination swirling within me. In the operating room, the surgical team buzzed around me, their movements swift and precise, like a well-oiled machine ready to tackle the task at hand. Dr. Lee's voice was steady as he began the procedure, each word a thread weaving through the fabric of my anxiety.

"We're going to repair the damage to your spleen and liver. It's going to be a long surgery, but we'll get through it together." His assurance washed over me like a warm wave, anchoring me in the reality that I wasn't alone.

Romeo's voice echoed in my mind, a mantra of reassurance, "Tutto andrà bene, amore mio."

The anesthesiologist's voice was soothing, a lullaby to my fraying nerves. "Mia, count backward from ten. Dieci, nove, otto..."

My eyes fluttered closed as the anesthesia took hold, pulling me into a realm of darkness where pain couldn't reach me, a peaceful escape from the chaos of reality.

Hours passed, and the surgical team worked tirelessly to repair the damage, their hands moving with precision, focused solely on my fragile body, while the world outside faded into oblivion.

Finally, the surgery was complete. Dr. Lee's face relaxed, a hint of a smile gracing his lips as he emerged from the operating room, the weight of the world visibly lifted from his shoulders.

"She's going to be okay," he whispered to Romeo, who had been waiting anxiously outside, his expression a tempest of worry and hope.

Tears welled in Romeo's eyes as he entered the recovery room, his breath hitching at the sight of me lying there, my face pale but my chest rising and falling with steady breaths.

"Amore mio," he whispered, his voice trembling with emotion, the relief washing over him like a tidal wave. "You're safe now."

Days turned into a blur, each moment stitched together with fragments of strength and hope. Romeo was by my side every step of the way, his love a constant source of comfort as I navigated the turbulent waters of recovery.

Together, we began to piece my life back together, one small step at a time, finding beauty in the most mundane moments. And with every shared smile, every whispered promise, I could feel the shackles of my past slowly crumbling, allowing the light to seep back into my life.

Finally, the morning arrived when Dr. Lee entered the room with a grin, his eyes bright with news. "Mia, we've got great news. You're free to go home."

Romeo's eyes lit up with joy, his smile stretching from ear to ear as he clasped my hand. "Amore mio, we're going home!"

The world outside beckoned, filled with possibilities and dreams that had once seemed distant but now felt within reach.

And as we left the sterile walls of the hospital behind, hand in hand, I couldn't help but feel that the darkest days were finally behind us. Together, we would face whatever came next, with love as our guiding light.

"How much do you want Daddy to take you to the world of darkness, where the shadows will consume you, and the only light will be the fire that burns between us, my prettiest whore."

"Everything," I begged like a needy whore that I was for him.

He sighed as he pulled my head back and looked into my eyes, smirking at the way that I loved it. I reveled in every sensation he gave me, even when it hurt.

The pleasure was sublime, a delicious ache that left me breathless. His kisses were voracious, filled with a hunger that I eagerly satisfied. I felt alive, electric, as his touch sparked a fire within me.

He refused to remove the drip, fearing more complications, but that didn't stop him from indulging in my body. He lavished attention on me, his skilled hands coaxing out every ounce of pleasure. I felt like an instrument in his hands, played to perfection. As he explored my body, I knew I was at his mercy.

And I wouldn't have it any other way. His touch was a symphony of sensations, a harmony of pleasure and pain that left me gasping for more. Romeo sat down but before he did, he took off his cock from his tracks. Without wasting more time, I dragged my hospital gown up before removing my thong.

"You succeeded, right, my sexy whore", he asked me.

"Yes, Daddy, I did, and I am so happy," I said. "Your little slut got what you wanted and now it is all mine".

I could feel the wetness of my pussy juices flowing down on my thighs and all I could think of was his cock in me. It was as if my pussy had missed him and all kept rushing like a person on drugs.

I could feel my pussy twitch at every second as I moved my hips and put his cock against my entrance. Romeo slammed into me without saying anything.

He instinctively thrust his cock, which reached the deepest part of me. I could feel it in my stomach. It was as if his cock had grown much bigger than the last time.

Come on, what was I saying when we had sex thrice in a row? His cock kept sliding in and out of my cunt. I begged him to fuck me harder, and he obliged and gave it to me, which excited me as he fucked me like a sweet slut that I was for him.

I blushed as he praised me as I took his cock sliding in and out of my hole. I guided him more into my pussy as a droplet of my pussy juices ran down onto his cock.

All I could see was him sending me beyond the heavens and god, his girth was voluptuous.

"I love this, Daddy", I purred.

I battled my eyelashes and asked him,

"Daddy can you fuck me like this always. "And all he did was kiss my neck before licking it like the crazy, obsessed man that he was for me.

I rode him hard and fast, as my body was against his.

"Ahhhhh", I kept moaning. Forgetting that we were in the hospital. I didn't know how I would face the hospital people tomorrow, as all I did was keep screaming and moaning from the intense pleasure that I felt.

Romeo grasped my breasts through the hospital dress that I wore. He removed it and eagerly sucked on it. He gave each of them the attention they deserved and pinched them hard.

My nipples grew harder, and I quivered as he sucked them like he was hungry for them.

"You are so tight, my angel", he purred. I was full of pleasure and desire as we gazed at each other. Our eyes matched with ours, and we were lost in the moment. Romeo violently thrust into me, and all that was heard was the echoes of our lovemaking.

My back arched as I shook from the intense pleasure felt on his cock. He held my neck as he continued to thrust into me roughly.

He kept thrusting more powerfully into me and the pressure from his cock was magnificent. I was a whore and I accepted it all. If I were getting it from the man that I loved and hadn't confessed to him that I love him before the incidents that occurred.

I saw stars and was out of control with my coming on his cock. I lost count of the times that I came, or I couldn't recall how long I came, but what made it possible was the pleasure that I got from his girth.

His cock throbbed inside me as he finally thrust before spilling his semen into me. Pure pleasure consumed me, and I moaned without a care in the world. We kissed as he dropped every drop before removing his cock from me.

We lay entwined on the bed, wrapped in each other's arms, our bodies speaking a language that words couldn't express.

The silence was palpable, yet eloquent, a symphony of sighs, whispers, and gentle murmurs. Our hearts beat as one, our love a living, breathing entity that pulsed through every fiber of our being.

In that moment, nothing else mattered. No words were needed, no explanations or declarations.

Our love was a silent understanding, a deep connection that transcended language. We simply existed, lost in the warmth of each other's embrace, our souls entwined forever.

CHAPTER TWENTY-THREE

MIA BIANCHI

The door swung open, and I stepped into the sunlight, the world outside feeling like a distant dream I was finally waking up to. The warmth of the sun kissed my skin, and for a brief moment, it felt like I could let go of the weight I'd been carrying, a stark contrast to the sterile, cold environment I had just left behind.

Romeo, ever steady, took my hand, his grip firm and reassuring, grounding me in this moment of transition. "You got this, amore mio. We'll face this new chapter together," he said, his voice a steady anchor amidst the whirlwind of uncertainty that still swirled in my mind.

As we walked toward the car, the campus stretched before me. The familiar buzz of activity had changed, the faces unfamiliar, the energy different, but still filled with life. I could feel the weight of the world lifting slightly as I stepped further away from the hospital, but there was an undeniable knot in my stomach. The thought of returning to a normal routine—whatever that meant now—was both comforting and daunting.

The air, though warmer than I had expected for this time of year, was invigorating. The breeze tugged at the edges of my hair, the fragrance of fresh grass and earth wrapping itself around me. I breathed in deeply, trying to center myself, trying to believe that this was happening—that I was really free.

Romeo squeezed my hand, pulling me back into the present moment. "You've already come so far. Let's just take it one step at a time," he murmured, his smile soft but full of conviction.

As we made our way across the bustling campus, the sounds of students laughing and talking seemed so distant, as though I were hearing them through a haze. I couldn't help but feel out of place, like an outsider peering into a world I didn't quite fit into anymore. My heart raced, my breath catching as I passed through the gates of the campus grounds.

The building loomed before me, and I hesitated for a moment before pushing open the heavy doors of the auditorium. The vastness of the space hit me instantly, the high ceilings, the rows of seats stretching endlessly before me. It felt both intimidating and exhilarating, a reflection of what I was about to face—an entirely new journey that I had no idea how to navigate.

Professor Thompson, a familiar face in this sea of strangers, greeted me with a warm, reassuring smile that seemed to light up the room. His presence was like a quiet comfort amid my swirling emotions. "Welcome back, Mia. We're so glad to have you," he said, his voice soothing, the kindness in it like a balm for my frayed nerves.

"Thanks, Professor. I'm ready to catch up," I replied, forcing a smile, though I could feel the weight of my uncertainty hanging around my words.

After the lecture, I sought out Mrs. Patel, my academic advisor, her kind eyes scanning me as she greeted me with a soft hug. "Mia, you've been through so much. Please don't push yourself too hard," she advised gently, concern deep in her voice.

"I won't, Mrs. Patel. I promise," I said, my words more certain than I felt, my heart pounding with the intensity of my determination. "I just want to get back on track."

She smiled, her warmth easing some of the tension that had built up inside me. "I know you do. Let's work together to create a plan that helps you balance your coursework and recovery."

Next came a group project meeting, and the nerves settled back into my chest. The thought of interacting with new classmates made me uneasy, but I clung to Romeo's words, his unshakeable faith in me like armor around my fragile confidence.

As I entered the meeting room, a chorus of cheerful greetings greeted me, and I found myself swept into a welcoming embrace of friendly faces. A girl with a bright smile caught my attention, her energy so infectious that it immediately put me at ease.

"Hey, I'm Sophia! Welcome to the team!" she exclaimed, her enthusiasm contagious.

"Thanks, Sophia. I'm Mia," I said, my voice steadier now, feeling a small spark of connection ignite in the pit of my stomach.

The meeting was a blur of ideas and brainstorming, each voice around the table sparking new thoughts and ideas. As the conversations unfolded, I found myself contributing with more ease than I expected, each word coming more naturally as the collective energy of the group fueled my own.

When the meeting finally concluded, I stepped outside to find Romeo waiting for me, his presence a grounding force in the whirlwind of my day. He smiled as I approached, his pride and admiration evident in his eyes. "Amore mio, you're doing great. I knew you could do it," he said, enveloping me in a warm embrace that melted away the remnants of my anxiety.

"Grazie, Romeo. I couldn't have done it without you," I said, my heart swelling with gratitude. His unwavering support was the anchor I needed to stay steady in this unfamiliar world.

Over the next few days, I threw myself into my work, balancing lectures, meetings with professors, and endless assignments. Every moment, Romeo was by my side, offering encouragement and support. He brought me coffee, his smile lifting my spirits even on the most difficult days.

One afternoon, as I sat in the library, struggling to focus on an assignment, Sophia approached us, her eyes bright with curiosity. "Hey, Mia, Romeo, mind if I join you?" she asked, her voice full of friendly enthusiasm.

"Of course, Sophia," I said, grateful for the company. The weight of solitude lifted as she joined us, her presence a reminder that I wasn't alone in this journey.

As we studied, Sophia glanced at me, her concern apparent as she met my eyes. "So, how's your recovery going?" she asked softly, her voice filled with genuine care.

I hesitated, unsure of how much to share, but Romeo's steady presence gave me the courage to speak. "It's been tough," I admitted, my voice trembling with the vulnerability I hadn't expected to feel. "But I'm determined to get back on track."

Sophia nodded, her expression filled with understanding. "You're doing great, Mia. We're all rooting for you."

I smiled, feeling a warmth spread through me at her words. "Thanks, Sophia. That means a lot."

Romeo squeezed my hand, his pride and admiration shining through his gaze. "Amore mio, you're doing amazing," he said, his voice full of love and pride.

CHAPTER TWENTY-FOUR

MIA BIANCHI

I walked into the library, a sense of purpose and anticipation swelling within me like the tide rising against a shore. The cool, slightly musty air was infused with the scent of old pages and polished wood. Sunlight filtered through the tall windows, casting a warm glow over the rows of books that stood like sentinels, guarding knowledge and stories waiting to be uncovered.

My academic routine was finally falling into place, and with each passing day, I felt my confidence blossoming, nourished by my determination to reclaim my path.

Settling into my favorite corner, a cozy nook by a window overlooking the campus, the soft rustle of pages and distant whispers created a soothing soundtrack. Just then, Evra, my best friend and Romeo's sister, plopped down beside me, a stack of law books teetering precariously in front of her, threatening to spill like an overstuffed suitcase.

"Hey, girl! How's business admin treating you?" she asked, her bright smile lighting up the dimly lit space.

I returned her smile, grateful for the welcome distraction. "It's good, Evra. I'm finally getting the hang of it," I replied, a rush of relief flooding through me.

Evra nodded, her eyes flickering between her notes and me, determination etched on her features. "I'm glad to hear that. You're doing great, Mia," she encouraged, her tone warm and sincere.

As we studied, Evra shared anecdotes from her law school journey, her voice animated as she recounted her struggles with tort law and the overwhelming demands of her professors. I listened intently, appreciating her insight and encouragement, feeling the weight of her experience settle over me like a comforting blanket.

"What struck me most was her perspective on my relationship with Romeo. 'You two are adorable, but don't forget to prioritize your own goals and aspirations, okay?

You have so much potential, Mia," she said, a hint of seriousness creeping into her playful demeanor.

A wave of gratitude washed over me. "Thanks for looking out for me. I promise I won't lose sight of my own goals," I assured her, feeling a renewed sense of commitment to my aspirations.

Evra's eyes sparkled with warmth, her smile reassuring. "I know you won't, Mia. You're strong and capable. And I'll always be here to remind you of that," she promised, a bond of friendship solidifying between us.

After a long day of classes, Evra suggested we take a break. "Hey, Mia, I need a breather from law books. Want to join me for coffee?" Her invitation felt like a lifeline, a chance to step away from the academic grind.

I eagerly agreed, and together we made our way to a cozy coffee shop near campus. The bell above the door jingled cheerfully as we stepped inside, and the rich aroma of freshly brewed coffee enveloped us, instantly lifting my spirits. We found a quiet corner to settle in, the soft hum of conversation around us creating a soothing backdrop that encouraged us to relax.

Over steaming cups of cappuccino, Evra leaned in, her curiosity evident as she sipped her drink. "How was business school today?" she inquired, her eyes bright and attentive.

I filled her in on my classes, my excitement bubbling over as I recounted the highlights of my day. She reciprocated by sharing her tales from law school, our conversation flowing easily as we lost ourselves in the discussion, laughter dancing between us like sunlight on water.

With a heartfelt smile, I turned to Evra. "Thanks for being such an amazing friend. Your guidance and support mean everything to me," I said, my voice earnest.

Evra's eyes softened, her expression warm and genuine. "Anytime, Mia. We're in this together," she reassured, her words enveloping me like a protective shield.

We spent the next hour studying, discussing our respective courses, and exchanging stories about our professors. Evra regaled me with tales of her toughest moments in law school, from grueling exams to demanding professors.

"I thought I was going to lose my mind during torts," she said, laughter bubbling up as she remembered. "But I survived, and you will too."

I nodded, feeling a sense of solidarity. "I know, right? Business school can be just as brutal," I replied, sharing in her relief and camaraderie.

As we delved deeper into our studies, Evra offered words of wisdom, her experience shining through. "Remember, Mia, it's not just about the grades—it's about learning, growing, and staying true to yourself." Her voice was like a gentle compass, guiding me through the fog of uncertainty.

I smiled, grateful for her insight. "You're the best, Evra," I replied, feeling uplifted.

In a lighthearted moment, Evra teased me about my newfound business jargon. "Mia, you're speaking corporate again. Translate, please!"

I playfully rolled my eyes, a laugh escaping my lips. "Sorry, Evra. I'll try to keep it simple," I said, enjoying the banter that had become a staple of our friendship.

As the evening drew to a close, I felt a surge of vulnerability and decided to confide in Evra about my relationship with Romeo. "I'm so happy, Evra, but sometimes I worry about losing myself in the process," I admitted, my heart racing as I laid bare my fears.

Evra listened intently, her expression empathetic. "You won't, Mia. You're strong, capable, and loved. Just remember to prioritize yourself, too," she advised, her tone a comforting balm to my anxiety.

With her words echoing in my mind, I felt a sense of triumph, knowing I had Evra's unwavering support every step of the way. As we finished our coffee, Evra glanced at her watch, the reality of her busy schedule returning.

"I have to run, Mia. I have a study group meeting in 20 minutes," she said, a hint of regret in her voice.

I nodded, gathering my things. "I should get going, too. I have a paper to finish," I replied, the weight of responsibility settling on my shoulders.

We hugged tightly, the warmth of our friendship wrapping around us like a comforting blanket. "Thanks again, Evra. You're the best," I said, feeling a swell of appreciation.

Evra smiled, her eyes shining with sincerity. "Anytime, Mia. We're in this together," she reiterated, the promise of our friendship echoing in my heart.

The next day, I found Evra in the library, surrounded by stacks of law books that seemed to threaten to topple over at any moment. I smiled, remembering our heartfelt conversation from the day before.

"Hey, Evra. How's it going?" I asked, genuinely curious.

She looked up, exhaustion flickering in her eyes but a smile gracing her lips. "It's going. Just trying to survive law school," she said, her voice tinged with a mix of determination and fatigue.

I nodded sympathetically, the shared struggle uniting us. "I know the feeling. But we'll get through it together," I reassured her, a sense of camaraderie enveloping us.

Evra's smile brightened, her expression softening with appreciation. "Thanks, Mia. That means a lot to me," she replied, her gratitude palpable.

With that, we dove back into our studies, ready to face whatever challenges lay ahead, side by side, our spirits intertwined like the pages of the books surrounding us.

CHAPTER TWENTY FIVE

MIA BIANCHI

I walked through campus, my backpack weighing heavily on my shoulders, textbooks and notes crammed together like a reminder of the pressure I was under. It was my final semester, a time that should have felt like a victory lap, but instead, I found myself consumed by a gnawing sense of unease. The presence of Jamie still loomed over me like a storm cloud, casting a shadow that made it difficult to breathe.

Despite the constant bustle of students passing by—chatter, laughter, and the frantic energy of a campus in full swing—I couldn't shake the isolation that clung to me. I glanced over my shoulder more than once, half-expecting to see him lurking in the shadows of the quad, waiting for his next move.

I was lost in these thoughts when, out of nowhere, Romeo appeared, slipping his arms around me from behind and pulling me close. His warmth grounded me, offering a brief moment of safety amid the chaos of my mind. "You're safe, Mia. I promise," he murmured, his breath warm against my ear. "Sei al sicuro, amore mio."

The calmness in his voice washed over me like a gentle tide, easing the tension that had built up. Still, the image of Jamie's menacing grin haunted me, sending an involuntary shiver down my spine.

The sudden shift of focus to Marco and Leo kept the unease alive but allowed for the introduction of new elements.

Just as I was finding comfort in Romeo's embrace, two towering figures emerged from the crowd. Marco and Leo. They were like shadows, standing by me as if they were always there, despite not having been introduced yet. Their presence was like a silent storm brewing on the horizon. Romeo introduced them, his voice steady and calm, but I could feel the tension building inside me.

"Romeo, I don't need babysitters!" I snapped, the frustration in my chest spilling out. The air felt colder, the crunch of the fallen leaves beneath my feet accentuating the sharpness of my words.

Romeo didn't flinch, his calm gaze locking onto mine. "Mia, please understand. This is for your protection. Jamie's still out there, and I won't risk losing you." His voice softened, and he added, "Non posso perderti, Mia."

I looked into his eyes, seeing the fear there, the same fear that had been swirling inside me for weeks. The realization hit me that he wasn't just being overprotective; he was scared. And maybe, just maybe, I was too. I finally relented, the fight leaving me as I silently acknowledged the truth of his words. Marco and Leo, standing guard at a distance, became a symbol of the danger we both feared— an ever-present reminder of what we were up against.

The following shift to routine and quieter moments helped build a smoother bridge to the intimate moments shared between Mia and Romeo, adding depth to their connection.

As the days blurred into one another, Romeo's visits became a constant. Each day, he was there, like a lighthouse in the storm of my hectic life. He'd help me with my studies or just be a reassuring presence, and before long, his presence didn't just feel comforting—it became necessary.

One afternoon, he walked into the library with that familiar warm smile, and for a fleeting moment, everything else faded away. "Hey, bella. How's it going?"

"Just trying to survive this semester," I replied, the exhaustion creeping into my voice, but his smile always had a way of lifting the weight off my shoulders.

Romeo's concern was evident, but his smile never wavered. "You're doing great, Mia. I'm proud of you. Sei fantastica, Mia. Sono così orgoglioso di te."

Those words those words filled with such sincerity, made me feel like maybe I could do this. Maybe I could get through the rest of the semester with him by my side.

The connection between us deepened as we studied together. The library became our sanctuary, the quiet hum of focus wrapping around us as we shared these small, precious moments. Romeo, ever patient, would help me with concepts I struggled with, his guidance bringing me back to the present when my thoughts wandered back to Jamie. But with Romeo next to me, I could breathe a little easier. I wasn't alone in this.

His kisses trailed down my neck, each soft brush of his lips sending tingling sensations along my spine. I closed my eyes, surrendering to the sensations swirling around us— his warmth, the intoxicating scent of his cologne, the intoxicating mix of urgency and longing that enveloped us.

In that moment, nothing else mattered. Not Jamie, not the shadows that threatened to encroach on our happiness— only the two of us, entwined in this dance of passion and trust. I felt liberated, as if every kiss was a chain breaking, every touch a promise of freedom from the suffocating weight of my past.

"Promise me you'll always be this real," I whispered, pulling back slightly to gaze into his deep, expressive eyes. "That you'll always be honest with me."

"Always," he vowed, the earnestness in his voice resonating deep within me. "You have my word, Mia. I'll never let anyone hurt you again."

With those words, I felt a sense of safety, a foundation to build upon, as if we were forging our destiny together, one kiss at a time. I knew that whatever darkness awaited us, we would face it side by side, fortified by the unbreakable bond we were crafting in this moment.

As we lost ourselves in each other, I understood that this was just the beginning of something profound—an adventure filled with passion, trust, and an unyielding commitment to one another.

And as the evening unfolded around us, I felt the shadows of my past begin to fade, eclipsed by the brilliant light of our love, and I realized that with Romeo by my side, I could face anything.

He spanked my bottom cheeks and I gasped and he continued which made my pussy clench and I tensed in anticipation of what was next to come. When Romeo was pleased with how red my cheeks were, he made me get on all fours.

And all I did was gaze at him with wanton eyes.

"Apri le gambe, mia dolce angelo," Romeo commanded, his voice low and husky. ("Spread your legs, my sweet angel.")

He paused, his eyes burning with desire. "Mostra a Papà cosa vuole vedere." ("Show Daddy what he wants to see.") I felt a thrill run through me as I obeyed, my heart racing with anticipation.

Romeo's gaze was like a caress, his eyes drinking in every inch of me. "Ah, mia bella," he whispered, his voice full of awe. ("Ah, my beauty.")

He reached out a trembling hand, his fingers tracing the curves of my body. I felt like a work of art, a masterpiece created just for him.

And in that moment, I knew I was his, completely and utterly. And I did without any form of disobedience. There was a smile on his face as I widened my legs more for him.

He looked at my cunt as it leaked and dripped down my inner thighs. I enjoyed the way he made me feel, and there wasn't a single doubt about it. He moved his fingers on my little bud as it glistened in the light.

Indicating my aroused self. "Tutte queste sono mie, Mia," Romeo declared, his voice low and possessive. ("All of these are mine, Mia.")

He paused, his eyes burning with passion.

"Le tue labbra, la tua pelle, le tue curve... ogni centimetro di te appartiene a me." ("Your lips, your skin, your curves... every inch of you belongs to me.")

Then he switched to English, his voice still dripping with desire. "Your heart, your soul, your every thought... I claim them all as my own."

Romeo's gaze held mine, his eyes burning with intensity.

"Sei mia, completamente e totalmente," he whispered in Italian, his voice husky with emotion. ("You are mine, completely and totally.")

I felt a shiver run down my spine as he spoke, his words echoing deep within me. I knew I was his, and I wouldn't have it any other way.

Before leaning down to kiss my forehead and lips. He moved my fingers in and out of my cunt and I thrashed as I moaned loudly. I loved the way my pussy made squishy sounds as he fingered me.

Romeo became a wild beast as if there was a switch in him and before I knew it, he spanked my pussy lips. It became swollen, full of pain, and pleasure, and wet with my arousal. I loved it and enjoyed the sensation that it gave.

I was such a good girl for him and was happy with the reward that I got from it. My nipples hardened, and my body was full of a traitorous arousal. I was impossibly wet and never wanted it to end.

He pushed down the jeans down his hips and revealed the cock that I wanted. The girth was so hard and thicker as the bulbous head bobbed towards me, and drops of pre-come dropped.

I licked my lips and yearned to take him inside my mouth. Romeo kneeled in front of my pussy as his mouth enclosed on it. He teased my mound as he licked it and my nipples erected painfully and my pussy felt empty as it needed his tongue sliding in and out of my pussy.

I shook with need as my pussy juices dripped down and he sucked my pussy like he was hungry for me. He blew on it as I moaned and dragged his fingers in and out of my cunt. He stoop up without wasting much time and placed his cock head against my entrance.

 I shivered with a wanton need as his length thrust in deep, and my body, despite the number of times we had sex. Still struggled to accommodate him and stretched around his cock. Romeo wasn't slow or gentle but he fucked me hard without mercy.

Like a slut and I took it all. In and out, he took me, his fingers digging into my flesh and marking me as his own. I shivered as the desire took over, and the passionate burn came as I moaned with pleasure.

His massive girth fucked me with fervor and I trembled with need and came apart each moment. He circled my clit and stroked it as his cock kept fucking me and I bucked wild as he pinched it.

Screaming, I rolled my hips as he kept pinching my clit.

"Come for me again, my sweetest little girl," he commanded me.

And I roared, coming as the cloud of sensation blinded me, and I shook heavily from it. His hips pistoned in and out as he fucked me rough and hard and I moved higher into the throes of orgasm.

We lost count of the exertion of his girth taking me harder and higher in the abyss of the shadows, and before I knew it. His cock throbbed suddenly, as I came harder nearly fainting.

Breathless, he pulled out of me and I squirmed as I missed his cock inside me. The essence of his semen leaked from me, and luckily for me.

Staying alone in the apartment was a wise decision, considering the passionate nights I shared with Romeo. I couldn't imagine facing my flatmates after our intense, scream-filled encounters.

The mere thought of it made me blush. As exhaustion took over, Romeo gently kissed my cheek, and we drifted off to sleep. Tomorrow was a school day, and I wondered how I would make it to class, considering the state I was in.

But I knew this wasn't the end of our love-making escapades. Far from it.

"Domani sarà un'altra giornata," Romeo whispered in my ear as if reading my thoughts. ("Tomorrow will be another day.")

And with that, we succumbed to slumber, our hearts still racing with the thrill of anticipation. The promise of what was to come lingered in the air like a sweet whisper, teasing us with the possibilities.

"Con questo, ci addormentammo," Romeo whispered, his voice barely audible. ("And with that, we fell asleep.")

But even as we slept, our hearts remained entwined, beating as one with an excitement that bordered on reverence. For we knew that tomorrow would bring another day of passion, of love, of us.

"E domani?" I wondered, my mind drifting off into the realm of dreams. ("And tomorrow?") Only time would tell, but one thing was certain - we couldn't wait to find out.

CHAPTER TWENTY-SIX

MIA BIANCHI

I woke up early on graduation day, the golden light filtering through my curtains, casting a warm glow across my room. My heart raced with a mix of excitement and nervousness, a thrilling tension coiling within me. This was the day I'd worked so hard for, the culmination of years filled with late nights, relentless studying, and a hope that had blossomed amidst the challenges.

Yet, even amid all the joy surrounding me, a lingering fear clung to my thoughts—Jamie. His shadow loomed in my mind, threatening to overshadow the happiness I longed to embrace, a dark cloud hovering over this momentous occasion.

As I stood by the window, lost in a whirlwind of emotions, I felt the familiar warmth of Romeo behind me. He wrapped his arms around my waist, pulling me close, his presence a comforting anchor in the storm of my anxiety.

"You're safe, Mia. I promise," he whispered, his breath warm against my ear, sending a ripple of reassurance through me. "Today is about celebrating your achievement." His voice was both soft and firm, filled with the kind of assurance that wrapped around me like a warm blanket. "Sei al sicuro, Mia. Ti amo."

Leaning back into him, I let the comfort of his words wash over me, allowing myself to believe in the safety he offered. I wanted to shake off the anxiety that clung to me like a second skin, but Jamie's presence was an unwelcome ghost, lurking at the edge of my thoughts.

The day unfolded in a blur of excitement and celebration. My family and Romeo's family arrived, their faces beaming with pride and love. I spotted my mom in the crowd, tears glistening in her eyes as she enveloped me in a tight embrace.

"We're so proud of you, Mia!" she exclaimed, her voice thick with emotion, her warmth enveloping me like a soft hug that melted away some of my worries.

As we took our seats for the ceremony, my gaze wandered to Evra in the audience. She was also graduating today, and we exchanged a glance that conveyed a mixture of excitement and nervousness. It was a big day for both of us, and I could feel the thrill vibrating between us, a shared acknowledgment of the journey that had led us here.

When my name was finally called, I took a deep breath, the weight of the moment settling on my shoulders like a heavy mantle. I walked across the stage, my heart pounding with every step. From the corner of my eye, I saw Romeo watching me, his eyes filled with an intense pride that made my heart swell.

"Ti amo, Mia," he whispered as I passed by, his voice like a soft melody that resonated in my heart. The applause and cheers from my family and loved ones rang in my ears, but all I could focus on was him and the warmth radiating from his presence. This moment belonged to both of us, and it felt as if time itself had paused, allowing me to savor the sweetness of the occasion.

After the ceremony, we celebrated with food, drinks, and laughter. Amid the festivities, Romeo surprised me with a thoughtful gift—a beautiful necklace adorned with a delicate graduation cap pendant, its shimmering silver catching the light.

"I'm so proud of you, Mia," he whispered as he fastened the necklace around my neck, his lips brushing against my ear, sending delightful shivers down my spine. "You deserve all the happiness in the world. Sei meravigliosa, Mia. Ti voglio bene."

As we danced and celebrated, I let myself revel in the love and support that surrounded me. For the first time in a long while, Jamie's shadow felt less suffocating. He was still out there, lurking in the periphery of my mind, but today was mine, and I was determined not to let him ruin it.

Later, Evra and I shared a special moment, both of us glowing with pride.

"We did it, girl!" she exclaimed, pulling me into a tight hug that felt like a burst of pure joy, her laughter blending seamlessly with the jubilant atmosphere.

Romeo approached, a bouquet in each hand, a thoughtful smile playing on his lips, brightening the moment further.

"Congratulations, bellas! You both deserve it," he said, handing each of us a bouquet and a small gift box. "Congratulazioni, belle! Meritate entrambe."

Inside my box, I found a stunning silver necklace with an even more intricate graduation cap pendant, tiny diamonds sparkling in the light. Evra's gift was an elegant watch, engraved with her initials. We both gasped at the beauty of the gifts, overwhelmed by his thoughtfulness.

"Wow, Romeo, thank you so much!" Evra said, clearly touched by his generosity, her eyes shining with appreciation.

Romeo smiled, but his gaze was locked onto mine, the depth of his gaze making my heart flutter with a mixture of warmth and longing.

"I have one more surprise for you, Mia. A private celebration, just for us," he said, his voice low and intimate, sending a delightful shiver down my spine. "Ho un'altra sorpresa per te, Mia. Una celebrazione privata, solo per noi."

My heart raced with anticipation as he took my hand, leading me away from the bustling crowd. We slipped into the night, away from the noise of the party, into the luxurious car that awaited us, the soft leather enveloping us in comfort.

Inside, the atmosphere was warm and intimate, the soft glow of candlelight illuminating a gourmet meal laid out before us. We feasted, laughter filling the space as our chemistry intensified with every shared glance and touch, our hearts dancing to an unspoken rhythm that felt electric.

As the night drew to a close, Romeo took my hand in his, his eyes dark with desire, igniting a spark within me.

"One more surprise, Bella," he murmured, his voice smooth as silk, the anticipation thickening in the air. "Un'altra sorpresa, bella."

He led me to a secluded cabin nestled deep in the forest, the cool air wrapping around us as the trees stood tall, creating a protective cocoon. The cabin itself exuded warmth, its rustic charm enhanced by the flickering glow of the fireplace inside. Soft candlelight danced across the walls, and the scent of fresh flowers lingered in the air, wrapping around us like a comforting embrace.

"This is our private sanctuary," Romeo whispered, his eyes never leaving mine, filled with a warmth that made my heart soar. "Il nostro santuario privato."

We sat down to a candlelit dinner, our hands brushing together frequently, each gentle touch sending sparks racing through me. Romeo's eyes burned with adoration, and his gaze was so intense that it felt like I was the only person in the world.

"Ti amo, Mia," he whispered, his lips grazing my ear as he pulled me closer, his voice imbued with sincerity. "You deserve all the happiness in the world. Sei bellissima, Mia."

After dinner, we sat by the fire, wrapped in each other's arms, the flames casting a soft glow on our faces. The warmth of the fire mirrored the heat of our shared connection, and the silence was broken only by Romeo's gentle voice.

"I'm so proud of the strong, beautiful woman you are," he whispered, his hand gently stroking my hair, sending waves of warmth through me. "Ti voglio bene, Mia."

In his arms, I felt an overwhelming sense of safety, as if I had finally found my place in a chaotic world. The chaos of the past few months, the danger, the fear—it all faded away in this serene moment, leaving only the echo of his heart beating against mine.

But as we held each other, the unspoken tension between us grew palpable. The passion that had simmered beneath the surface for so long could no longer be ignored.

"C'è stato troppo tempo, amore mio," Romeo whispered, his voice thick with longing, as if every word was a confession. "It's been too long, my love."

My heart raced in response, each beat resonating with the truth of his words. "Sì, è tempo di ravvivare la fiamma," I agreed, my voice trembling with desire, a confession of my own.

In that moment, the outside world ceased to exist. It was just Romeo and me, lost in each other, the air around us charged with anticipation. The passion that had been building between us finally ignited, consuming us in a whirlwind of desire, an inferno that refused to be contained.

Romeo's hands explored my body, his touch sending fire coursing through my veins, igniting every nerve ending.

The intensity of his gaze left me breathless as he whispered, "Sei mia, ora e sempre."

I surrendered completely, knowing that I was his, and he was mine—now and forever. In that cozy cabin, under the ethereal glow of the moonlight, we gave ourselves to each other fully, our love burning brighter than ever before, illuminating the dark corners of our hearts.

His whispered words echoed in my mind long after the night had ended: "Ti amo, Mia. You are my everything."

"Ti desidero," I whispered, my voice husky with longing. ("I desire you.")

But then, in the warmth of our shared intimacy, the playful glint returned to his eyes, igniting a fire of a different kind.

"First, baby, you're going to suck my cock so hard that you are going to gag before I ever think of fucking that sweet pussy of yours," he ordered, his voice low and commanding.

My pussy clenched and tightened hard as I grew impossibly wet, an electric thrill coursing through me at his commanding words. I bit my lip, anticipation flooding my senses as I nodded, eager to please him, to explore the depths of our connection even further.

He leaned closer, his breath warm against my skin, igniting a fire that blazed hotter with each passing second. "Good girl," he murmured, his voice thick with desire, causing shivers to race down my spine. "I want to hear you moan for me, baby. I want you to forget everything else but the pleasure we're going to create together."

The weight of his gaze made my heart race, each beat resonating with the promise of what was to come. I shifted slightly, the heat of the moment enveloping us like a cocoon, heightening the intensity of my longing.

As I sank to my knees in front of him, I felt a rush of exhilaration mixed with a hint of nervousness. The world around us faded, leaving only the two of us in this intimate embrace. I took a deep breath, steadying myself, focusing solely on him—the way his body responded to my presence, the raw hunger in his eyes.

"Let me show you how much I desire you," I whispered, my voice thick with anticipation, as I leaned closer, ready to fulfill his command.

With each movement, I felt empowered, driven by the need to please him, to taste the passion that swirled between us. His fingers tangled in my hair, urging me closer, he tasted like a velvet chocolate cream that I wanted to savor every single time. Romeo tasted salty and sweet like a forbidden fruit, and I was never tired of it.

As I bobbed my head on his cock, Romeo gripped the back of my head and guided his cock deeper into my mouth as it hit the back of my throat.

I gagged around like a slut with drops of saliva fell on his cock. I enjoyed everything he gave to me as he moved his hips back and forth and pushed deeper, making sure that I took every inch of him. My mouth stretched around his cock as my tongue sucked his cock most deliciously.

He fucked my face, and I delighted in it as tears dropped as he fucked me harshly on his cock. My mouth ached as I took him, despite it being too difficult for me due to his massive size.

But nothing matters but to have the taste of his glorious deliciousness. As he kept fucking my face and mouth on his cock, his cock throbbed and Romeo groaned as he came and I took him all, swallowing every drop and not wasting any.

As I stood up with his help. I lay on the bed as he kneeled between my legs. He widened my legs as he dragged his fingers on my crotch, and his fingers glistened, and Romeo brought them into his mouth. He closed his eyes, and he tasted me and smiled when he opened them.

"You're so delicious, my angel, and I want to have another taste of you," he purred.

Romeo's fingers slid into my wet folds, and I moaned as I was very wet for him. I didn't know what had happened, but I became demented for Romeo, especially whenever we had sex.

The electric trills of pleasure consumed me as his fingers continued to master my body, and my hips rocked against his. I lost control of myself as he slipped his fingers further inside me.

My pussy tightened and clenched as he pumped in and out of me. His fingers fucked me, stretching in a favorable sensation, settling deep into my core. Hot arousal identified me as my hips met with his fingering.

"Papi, this feels so good," I moaned.

We always had sex but always felt like the first time and I came from the penetration and rough fucking from his fingers. The orgasm from it was uncontrollable and nearly blinded me. It elicited happiness within me.

"Ti piace ciò che vedi, mia più bella angelo?" Romeo mormorò, la sua voce bassa e suadente, come un dolce mormorio di piacere. "Do you love what you see, my prettiest angel?" Romeo murmured, his voice low and husky, like a gentle hum of pleasure.

His hands cupped my bottom cheeks as he kept slapping each cheek hard until it became red, and it stung as if it was a mixture of pain and pleasure that I felt.

But he didn't stop as he punished my cheeks, and I started feeling hotter. My pussy clenched and twisted hard with desire. The spanking or punishment shouldn't arouse me this much, but it did like a blazing fire that spread across my body. I didn't stop, and I took it all. Romeo moved his hands down to my pussy and spanked it so hard that I jumped. It was painful but pleasurable. I arched my back more than he kept spanking it.

He traced his fingers across his mark, looking at how beautiful it looked.

"So beautiful," he breathed. "You were made for me, my little one".

His fingers scraped the marks without wasting more time or teasing.

He placed his cock over the top of my cunt and my needy bud clenched as it wanted the most tempting thing it wanted.

He used his length to stroke against my cunt as he grasped my waist and dug his fingers hard into me. A strangled moan escaped and without giving me any warning, Romeo slammed his cock deeper into my pussy.

He didn't give me any room for adjustment, as he moved roughly, faster, and harder. His cock kept forcing me from one orgasm to the other and it consumed me whole.

I cried out as my pussy juices slipped down my thighs and my pleasure intensified with every second that passed. He was master and commanded me whenever he wanted me to come on his cock.

And I obeyed as his length fucked me and my thighs quivered with every thrust taken. I was a losing mess, and I orgasmed and nearly slipped off, if it weren't for Romeo holding me.

I was desperate, and I kept begging him.

"Please, Papi, can I come?" My breath hitched at the back of my throat as he held my hair and throat and took everything from me.

I had power, and my core twisted in the dirtiest way ever. I was needy and my pussy convulsed at every praise he rendered. He circled my clit and fucked me raw and hard.

I couldn't as I hoarsely yelled and came so hard that all the strength that I had was Romeo finishing off. I was drained and exhausted, and luck was on my side.

When Romeo announced he was coming and came in me few minutes. His semen spread the insides of my inner cunt and Romeo pushed the ones that were out in.

That night was etched in my memory forever, a testament to the unbridled desire that consumed us. It was a night of unchained passion, of forbidden love that refused to be silenced.

Every moment was a declaration of our longing, a surrender to the fierce attraction that had been caged for so long. I yearned for more nights like that, where we could unleash our wildness and let our hearts run free.

And though I knew it wouldn't be the last time, I couldn't shake the feeling that our love was a fleeting dream, a moment of beauty that might vanish at any moment.

CHAPTER TWENTY-SEVEN

ROMEO GIUSEPPE

As I gazed into Mia's eyes, a wave of tranquility washed over me, like the gentle caress of a summer breeze. The cabin, nestled in the heart of the woods, enveloped us in its warmth, creating an intimate cocoon where time seemed to stand still. I knew, in that moment, I was exactly where I was meant to be. Our romantic getaway had been everything I'd hoped for—intimate, peaceful, and rejuvenating.

Each quiet moment we shared deepened our bond, weaving a tapestry of memories that felt unbreakable.

"Mia, ti amo," I whispered, my voice thick with emotion, each word laden with sincerity. "You make me feel alive."

Her heart melted at my confession, and she nestled closer into my arms, her warmth enveloping me like a comforting blanket on a chilly evening. Every inch of her felt like a piece of my soul, a reflection of my heart laid bare. I held her tighter, overwhelmed with gratitude for the love we shared—a love that felt destined, as if written in the stars.

The following day, excitement bubbled within me as I prepared a surprise for her—a romantic picnic in the park. I meticulously packed all her favorite foods, including a bottle of her cherished wine, my heart racing at the thought of her delight. Under the sprawling branches of a large oak tree, I lay out a beautiful blanket, the vibrant colors contrasting beautifully with the lush greenery around us. The air was crisp, infused with the earthy scent of nature, and the sky was a brilliant blue, dotted with fluffy clouds drifting lazily. Everything felt perfect, like a scene from a dream.

As we sat together, laughter spilling from our lips like music, Evra appeared, practically glowing with excitement. Her enthusiasm was infectious, drawing us into her orbit.

"Guys, I have amazing news! I got a job offer at a top law firm!" she exclaimed, her voice bursting with joy, eyes sparkling like stars in the night sky.

I immediately jumped to my feet, my heart swelling with pride for her accomplishment. "That's incredible, Evra! You deserve it!" I called out, my voice carrying my genuine excitement.

Mia hugged her best friend tightly, their smiles brightening the surroundings, their laughter ringing through the air like sweet chimes. The bond between them was palpable, a testament to their unwavering friendship. I felt a warmth spread through me, grateful to be part of this moment that celebrated their connection.

In the days that followed, I continued to stand by Mia's side, supporting her through every little challenge that came her way. Whether it was helping her navigate work pressures or lending an ear to her concerns, I wanted her to know that I was always there for her. I cherished the quiet moments, too—the ones where we would simply sit together, sharing our hopes and fears, as the world outside faded into oblivion.

As her birthday approached, the need to plan something special weighed on me. I wanted to create a memory that would forever echo in our hearts, a gesture that would illustrate just how much she meant to me. One evening, while we strolled along the beach, the waves gently lapping at our feet, I decided to bring it up.

"Mia, can I ask you something?" I said, looking down at her with a playful smile, my heart racing with anticipation.

"Of course, Romeo," she replied, curiosity dancing in her eyes, her voice light and inviting.

"What do you want to do for your birthday next week?" I asked, hoping to gauge her desires. I had a surprise in mind, but I wanted to hear her thoughts first.

Mia looked touched by my thoughtfulness, her expression softening. "I'm not sure... What did you have in mind?" she replied, tilting her head slightly, a playful glimmer in her gaze.

A grin spread across my face, mischief sparkling in my eyes. "It's a surprise. Trust me, you're going to love it." I could barely contain my excitement, the ideas swirling in my mind like a whirlwind of joy.

As we continued our walk, the sunset painted the sky in vibrant hues of pink and orange, casting a warm glow around us. The atmosphere felt electric, charged with unspoken words and shared dreams. I took Mia's hand, relishing the comfortable silence between us before speaking again.

"Mia, what's your favorite memory of us?" I asked, genuinely interested in her thoughts, eager to dive into the depths of her heart.

She paused, a soft smile spreading across her face as she reminisced. "I think it's our first date—when we went to the vineyard and watched the stars together. It felt magical, didn't it?"

I smiled, remembering that enchanting night, the way the stars had twinkled like diamonds against the inky sky. "That's one of my favorites too," I said, giving her hand a gentle squeeze, the warmth of her skin igniting sparks of affection within me.

As the weekend drew near, we began planning our getaway, our excitement palpable. I had my heart set on the beach, the soft sands calling to me, but Mia had other ideas.

"I think we should go to the mountains," she suggested, looking up at me with a hopeful expression, her eyes shimmering with dreams. "I need a break from the sun."

I raised an eyebrow, playfully protesting. "But I've been craving the beach for weeks. It's so relaxing, with the sound of waves crashing and the sun warming our skin," I argued, picturing the idyllic shoreline.

Mia sighed, her expression softening, as she gazed out at the horizon. "I know, but I'm not in the mood for sand and sunburn. Can't we compromise?" Her voice was gentle, yet firm, a plea I couldn't ignore.

I thought for a moment, considering her request. "How about a lake house? We can enjoy the water without the intense sun. Imagine sipping wine on the dock, surrounded by nature," I proposed, hoping to find a middle ground.

Her face lit up instantly, and her eyes sparkled with delight. "That sounds perfect!" she exclaimed, a grin breaking across her features, illuminating the surrounding evening.

"Great. I'll start looking for options," I replied, relieved that we'd found a compromise that made both of us happy.

As I searched for the ideal lake house, Mia cuddled up beside me on the couch, her head resting against my shoulder. "I'm so excited about our trip," she said, her eyes bright with enthusiasm, radiating joy that warmed my heart.

"Me too, bella. It's going to be the perfect getaway," I replied, the excitement bubbling within me like the effervescence of champagne.

After scouring for the perfect lake house—its weathered wood and stunning lakeside views—it felt like our upcoming adventure was shaping up to be everything we both needed. The house we chose was nestled away in the woods, its windows reflecting the soft hues of the evening sky. As we pored over maps and travel guides, our fingers intertwined, I couldn't help but feel a deep sense of contentment.

The air around us felt alive with anticipation, charged with our dreams and hopes. As the stars began to twinkle overhead that night, I knew this trip was going to bring us even closer together, forging memories that would linger long after the summer days faded into the backdrop of our lives.

"My sweetest angel, do you want Daddy to fuck you very hard today," I asked her.

And I nodded my head, my heart racing with desire, as I craved him just as fiercely as he craved me. Our eyes locked, the air thick with tension, as we both knew in that moment, we were irretrievably lost in each other.

"Daddy's got you today, little one," I whispered, my voice low and husky, sending shivers down my spine.

"You're all mine, and I'm going to take care of you like only Daddy can." My words dripped with possessiveness and promise, making my heart flutter in anticipation.

"Pápa ti prende cura oggi, piccolo mia," I added, my Italian words caressing me like a soft breeze.

As I spoke, my hands cradled her face, my thumbs stroking her cheeks with tender gentleness. My eyes burned with a fierce devotion, a love that was both captivating and unnerving. "Ti amo, e sarò sempre qui per te," I whispered, my voice trembling with emotion.

She felt like a precious gem in my hands, cherished and protected. In that moment, I knew that she was safe, that Daddy would shield her from the world and make everything okay.

My presence enveloped her, a warm embrace that soothed her soul.

"Sei al sicuro con me, piccola," he murmured, his Italian words reassuring me.

She felt like a little girl again, cared for and loved, with no worries or fears.

"Daddy's got you," I repeated, my voice a gentle reminder of my love and devotion.

"Papà è qui," I added, my Italian phrase a soothing balm to her heart.

And she knew, in that instant, that she was home.

"Yes, Papi," she answered.

She breathed. "I want you to fuck me so that I can come all over your cock," she begged me.

As she uttered those words, my eyes flashed with a fierce intensity, my gaze burning into mine like a wildfire.

My jaw clenched, and a low, primal growl rumbled from the depths of my throat, sending shivers coursing down my spine.

With a swift, possessive movement, my hands circled her neck, my fingers wrapping around my skin like a vice. My thumbs brushed against the pulse points, sending a thrill of excitement through her.

My grip was firm, yet gentle, a paradox that left her breathless. It was a clear declaration of dominance, a reminder that I was in control. The air seemed to vibrate with tension as I leaned in, my face inches from hers, my warm breath dancing across her skin.

She felt a surge of adrenaline, her heart racing in response to the primal energy emanating from me.

In that moment, she was acutely aware of the power dynamic between us. I was the master of my domain, and she was my willing captive. The sensation was both exhilarating and terrifying, leaving her wondering what I would do next.

Would I tighten my grip or release her from my grasp? The uncertainty only added to the thrill, leaving her suspended in a state of delicious anticipation.

She whimpered, her voice trembling with need, as she begged me,

"Please, Daddy... please." Her words were laced with desperation, her body craving my touch, my love.

"Per favore, Papà...ti prego," she added, her Italian pleas mixing with her English ones, revealing the depth of her longing.

My eyes flashed with desire, my gaze burning into hers.

"Shh, little one," I whispered, my voice husky with emotion. "Daddy's got you. I'll take care of you."

I pulled myself closer, my arms enveloping her in a warm embrace.

"Ti amo, piccola mia," I murmured, my Italian words soothing my soul.

As I held her, I felt her neediness melt away, replaced by a sense of safety, of being loved and cherished. I knew that Romeo would fulfill my desires, that he would give me what that she needed.

I moved closer, my eyes fixed on her with an unnerving intensity, like a predator stalking its prey. My steps were silent, deliberate, and calculated, exuding a sense of control and power.

The air seemed to vibrate with tension as he closed in, my presence suffocating yet exhilarating. My gaze burned with a fierce hunger, my pupils dilated with desire, as if I was ready to pounce and devour her whole.

She felt a shiver run down her spine, her heart racing in anticipation, like a rabbit caught in the cross-hairs of a hunter's scope.

Every step I took, every inch she gained, seemed to strip her of her defenses, leaving her vulnerable and exposed.

Yet, she couldn't help but be drawn to me, like a moth to a flame, helpless to resist the pull of my magnetic presence. In Italian, I whispered,

"Sei mia, piccola mia" - You're mine, my little one - my voice low and husky, sending shivers down her spine.

She knew that she was my prey, and I was ready to claim her. Her pussy was wet as it clenched and she pleaded with me but kept I teasing her.

As my hands swiftly lifted her dress, the fabric whispering against her skin, all her whimpering and begging ceased.

She was left standing vulnerable, clad only in the delicate lingerie that hugged her curves. The air was electric with tension, and she felt a rush of anticipation mixed with trepidation.

Then, my hands came down upon her cheeks, the impact sharp and stinging. The sound echoed through the air, leaving no room for complaint or protest. She was silenced, her voice caught in her throat as a mixture of pain and pleasure coursed through her.

In that moment, she was suspended in a state of sensory overload, unable to speak or move. All she could do was feel the burning sensation on her skin, the rush of blood to the surface, and the throbbing ache that lingered.

My hands lingered, my fingers tracing the outline of her cheeks, as if claiming ownership of her body. In Italian, I whispered,

"Sei mia, ora e per sempre" - You're mine, now and forever - my voice low and husky, sending shivers down her spine.

She knew she was mine, completely and utterly, her body and soul bound to my will.

Suddenly, she felt nervous as I cupped her pussy with my hands. My hands grasped her shoulders, my fingers digging into her skin as I spun her around and pushed her against the sleek, polished table inside my lakeside villa.

The wooden edge bit into her hips, a stark contrast to the softness of the plush rug beneath her feet. She felt the cool lake breeze whisper through the open windows, carrying the sweet scent of blooming flowers and the distant lapping of water against the shore.

As she gazed up at me, she couldn't help but think of the numerous houses I owned, each one a testament to my wealth and power. She had lost count, to be honest – the penthouse in the city, the beachfront mansion, the private island retreat... But this lakeside haven, with its serene views and secluded privacy, was perhaps her favorite.

My eyes burned with intensity, my gaze pinning her to the spot as I leaned in, my face inches from hers. She felt trapped, yet thrilled, her heart racing in anticipation of what was to come.

The table creaked beneath her, a subtle reminder of the force I had used to push her against it. She was at my mercy, and she knew it.

A husky moan escaped from my lips as he moved a single digit around my clit and my thighs trembled due to being excessively horny, need and tired from being teased. I was so aroused as my wetness dripped down my thighs, and my eyes held the intensity within them.

As I drew closer, the scent of my Bvlgari Man Wood Essence wafted around her, its sophisticated, woody aroma teasing her senses. The subtle notes of lavender and vanilla mingled with the warmth of amber, creating an intoxicating blend that left her breathless.

I watched as her heart raced when I smiled, my eyes crinkling at the corners, and my smirk grew wider. The cologne seemed to amplify my presence, making me even more commanding and irresistible to her.

She was entranced, her senses heightened, as I leaned in closer, my warm breath whispering against her skin. Her eyes locked onto mine, and I saw the desire burning within them.

I felt my heart rate quicken as I gazed at her, my hands squeezing her pussy as she moaned and I smirked briefly, before spanking her pussy very hard.

She cried and moaned as it stung before she got the intense pleasure that she always felt. She had a heated arousal, and she throbbed in the most needy and delicious manner.

Her arousal dripped down her inner thighs, and she managed to hold her panting breaths. My fingers slipped inside her folds and I fucked her aching clit as she mewled as I fingered me.

The mannerism of my rough and hard fingering was very compelling and she became wetter as my masterful fingers fingered her. She moaned as a needy and wanton whore.

"Do you like what I am offering, my little needy one?" I mused, my voice low and husky, my Italian accent dripping like honey.

"Ti piace quello che ti offro, mia piccola bisognosa?" I continued, my eyes burning with intensity, my words a gentle caress.

Her pink pussy was wetter than ever and my lips savaged her neck, my tongue licking and nipping at her skin like a man possessed, as she felt a rush of ecstasy.

My laughter, low and husky, sent shivers down her spine, the sound vibrating against her skin in a way that left her breathless. She couldn't believe how much she craved this, how much she loved every taste of me, every touch, every whispered promise.

My laughter grew louder, more manic, and she felt herself getting lost in the sound, in the sensation of my mouth on her skin. It was like nothing she had ever experienced before - and she knew, in that moment, that she was mine, completely and utterly.

My fingers twisted in her hair, pulling her closer as I claimed her lips with a fierce, possessive kiss. She felt consumed by the intensity of my desire, her senses overwhelmed by the pressure of my mouth on hers.

All she could do was cling to me, her nails digging deep into my back as she tried to anchor herself against the storm of emotions that I was unleashing. I squeezed her hands tight, my fingers intertwining with hers, before pulling back to peck a gentle kiss on her forehead.

The contrast between the ferocity of my kiss and the tenderness of my touch left her breathless, her heart racing with excitement.

I unfastened my pants and revealed my cock. Her pussy clenched down hard after seeing my cock like it was the first time. She swallowed hard as she took the size of my enormous girth and saw the drop of pre-come that fell.

Her mouth watered as she wanted to have a taste of my cock. She watched the way that I stroked my cock, my fingers gliding up and down, and she salivated.

Her pussy was wetter than before and all she wanted was a taste of on her lips. She kneeled in front of me as I made sure to use my cock to slap her face.

I held my hair and gripped it. My cock got much harder, and I groaned out. She was happy that she was the only one who made me feel that way.

"Ti piace quello che vedi, Mia?" I whispered, his voice husky and low. "You make me feel alive, bella. The way you look at me, the way you touch me... It's like a spark has been lit within me."

And all she did was moan, which clenched her pussy. She was full of need, and I wasn't making it easier for her. I just kept teasing her, and she knew that it was going to be worth it.

CHAPTER TWENTY-EIGHT

MIA BIANCHI

Mia Floré, my global perfume empire, was thriving beyond my wildest dreams. The sweet, intoxicating scents that filled my office whispered of success and hard work. Yet, amid the floral notes and citrus bursts that surrounded me, my mind was tangled in worry, much like the intricate patterns of the fragrances I crafted.

"Romeo, I'm feeling overwhelmed," I confessed, my voice trembling with anxiety, each word a fragile thread in the fabric of my thoughts. "The business is growing so fast, and I'm not sure I can keep up." The weight of responsibility pressed down on me like an anchor, threatening to pull me into the depths of uncertainty.

Romeo, seated across from me, took my hand in his, his grip warm and reassuring, grounding me in the moment. His emerald eyes met mine, filled with unwavering support that felt like a lifeline in the storm. "Amore, you're doing incredible. I'm so proud of you. You've built this empire from scratch, and it's only natural to feel stressed," he said, his voice steady, wrapping around my fears like a soft embrace.

Just then, Aurelio, Romeo's father, entered the room, his warm smile radiating a sense of comfort that enveloped me. "Mia, my dear, you're part of the family now. We're here to support you. Let us help you with the business," he offered, his voice steady and inviting, like the promise of dawn after a long night.

Evra, Romeo's sister, chimed in with enthusiasm, her eyes sparkling with excitement. "We're all in this together, Mia. You're not alone." Her words danced around me, igniting a flicker of hope in the shadow of my doubt.

As we discussed strategies and potential collaborations, I felt a growing sense of belonging, as though I had finally found my tribe amid the chaos. Their encouragement enveloped me like a warm embrace, igniting a fire within that I thought had dimmed. But just as I began to feel at ease, Romeo's phone buzzed, shattering the moment like glass.

"I'm sorry, amore. I need to take this. Work-related stress," he said, his expression shifting to one of seriousness as he stepped away to take the call. My heart skipped a beat, but I pushed the doubt aside, focusing on the love and acceptance surrounding me.

As the meeting concluded, relief washed over me, mingling with gratitude. The Giuseppes' support meant the world to me. Romeo returned, taking my hand again, his eyes locked on mine, filled with determination that matched the rhythm of my heart. "Amore, we're in this together. We'll make Mia Floré a global phenomenon," he assured me, his voice a soothing balm against my worries.

Aurelio smiled, pride palpable in his gaze. "We'll do everything to help you succeed, Mia. You're part of the family now." Evra nodded enthusiastically, her passion igniting my spirit. "We'll make it happen, Mia. Together."

My heart swelled with emotion as I looked at the people surrounding me, a familial warmth blossoming within. In that moment, I was reminded of my school days when Jamie, my then-boyfriend, had been a constant source of encouragement. He'd often pick me up from school, listening intently as I shared my dreams and aspirations.

One afternoon, as we strolled through the park, the sun casting a golden glow over everything, Jamie turned to me, his warm smile brightening the gloomy day. "Mia, I know you've been stressed lately. I'm here for you, and I want to help." His sincerity wrapped around me like a comforting blanket.

My heart swelled with gratitude, the kind that surged through your veins like a sweet elixir. "Thanks, Jamie. Just talking to you makes me feel better." I could feel the walls around my heart beginning to soften, allowing his kindness to seep in.

Evra and I had been meaning to catch up for weeks, but our busy schedules kept getting in the way. Finally, she sent me a text that felt like a lifeline: "Hey girl! I need a coffee break and some quality time with you. Free today?"

"Perfect timing! I could use a coffee and a chat. Let's meet at Sunny Grounds at 2?" I replied, the anticipation already lifting my spirits like the first rays of dawn breaking through the darkness.

Settling into the cozy café chair, I relished the warmth of the sunlight streaming through the window. The aroma of freshly brewed coffee filled the air, wrapping around me like a warm hug. Evra's gentle smile and concerned eyes made me feel safe, a haven from the turmoil inside me.

"Hey, love, what's going on?" she asked, her voice soft and soothing, an anchor in the storm of my thoughts. "You seem a little lost lately."

My gaze drifted downward, my fingers tracing the intricate patterns on my cup, the warmth grounding me in the moment, as if the simple act of holding the cup could stabilize my spiraling thoughts.

"I don't know, Evra. I just feel... stuck. Like I'm wandering through life without a purpose," I admitted, the weight of my vulnerability heavy in the air, a confession that felt both terrifying and freeing.

Evra's hand covered mine, offering a comforting squeeze that sent ripples of warmth through me. "You're not alone, Mia. We all feel that way sometimes. But what's bothering you? Is it work, or something deeper?" Her understanding gaze was a balm for my restless soul.

My eyes welled up, tears threatening to spill over like a fragile dam ready to break. "It's just... I feel like I'm living a lie. Like I'm pretending to be this strong, confident person, but inside, I'm still that scared, vulnerable girl." The confession hung in the air, heavy with the weight of my fears.

Evra's expression turned empathetic, her eyes shining with compassion. "Oh, Mia, you are strong and confident. But it's okay to be vulnerable too. That's where the real growth happens." Her words resonated within me, striking a chord I hadn't realized was so deeply buried.

As we talked, the café's gentle hum and the rich aroma of freshly brewed coffee enveloped us, creating a cocoon of warmth and security. I felt my walls slowly crumbling, allowing my true feelings to surface, like spring flowers pushing through the last remnants of winter snow.

I realized that I wasn't alone in my struggles and that true growth came from embracing vulnerability. With Evra by my side, I felt a sense of belonging and acceptance, as if I'd finally found my tribe.

With renewed determination, I stood up, my eyes locked on Evra's, a fire igniting within me. "Thank you for being here for me, Evra. I feel like I can face anything now."

Evra smiled, her eyes shining with warmth, reflecting the light of our friendship. "That's what friends are for, Mia. We're in this together, always."

I smiled back, a deep sense of gratitude and love swelling within me for this woman who had become like a sister. As we hugged goodbye, I knew that I still had a long way to go, but with the support of my loved ones and my inner strength, I was ready to face whatever challenges came my way.

Stepping out of the coffee shop, I inhaled deeply, the sun shining brightly, casting a warm glow over the bustling streets. I took a deep breath, letting the cool breeze fill my lungs. I knew that I would always carry the scars of my past with me, but I also understood that I had the power to create a brighter future.

With that thought invigorating me, I stepped forward, ready to face whatever lay ahead. Over the next few weeks, I threw myself into my work, using the lessons I had learned from Evra and my introspection to guide me.

I was determined to make Mia Floré a success, not just for myself, but for all the people who believed in me.

As I worked, I felt a sense of purpose and fulfillment that I had never known before, each fragrance I crafted weaving together my dreams and aspirations. I was finally living my truth, and it felt exhilarating.

Romeo and I grew closer, our bond strengthened by our shared struggles and triumphs. We became each other's rock, supporting and loving one another through thick and thin, our connection deepening like roots entwining beneath the surface.

Aurelio and Evra became like a second family to me, always offering guidance and encouragement whenever I needed it, their unwavering belief in me propelling me forward. Together, we navigated the complexities of the business, each challenge transforming into an opportunity for growth, much like the fragrances I poured my heart into.

With every step, I felt more grounded, ready to embrace whatever lay ahead, surrounded by love and support. I was no longer just Mia Floré—the woman behind the brand—I was a part of something greater, a tapestry woven with threads of resilience, passion, and unwavering friendship.

CHAPTER TWENTY- NINE

MIA BIANCHI

I sat in the kitchen, savoring the rich aroma of my coffee, the dark brew steaming in my cup like a comforting hug. The sun filtered through the large windows, casting a warm glow on the room and illuminating the polished countertops where Caroline moved gracefully, her hands deftly maneuvering through fresh ingredients as she expertly prepared lunch.

The rhythmic clatter of pots and pans harmonized with her light laughter, creating a symphony of warmth that wrapped around me like a cozy blanket on a chilly morning.

Just then, Romeo walked in, and time seemed to pause. His tall frame filled the doorway, the morning light framing him in a halo that made my heart race. Our eyes locked, and his warm smile ignited a flutter in my chest that sent tingles racing down my spine.

"Amore, I see you're getting to know Caroline," he said, his voice low and husky, reverberating in the intimate space between us. Each syllable wrapped around me, making me feel cherished and seen.

I nodded, feeling an effortless ease in Caroline's presence. "Yes, I was just asking her about her employment." My words felt like soft petals unfolding, revealing my curiosity and interest in the woman who was now part of our daily lives.

However, I noticed a subtle shift in Romeo's expression as he spoke, his brow furrowing slightly. "Luca handled the interviews. He found Caroline to be the best candidate." The seriousness in his tone contrasted with the lightness of the moment, casting a shadow over the cheerful atmosphere like a fleeting cloud blocking the sun.

Caroline nodded in agreement, her smile brightening the room like the sun breaking through clouds. "Yes, I was interviewed by Luca. He was... very professional." Her words carried an undertone of respect, and I couldn't help but notice the way her eyes sparkled when she mentioned

Luca, a hint of something deeper dancing behind her words.

I recalled Luca as Romeo's secretary, yet there was an unspoken connection between him and Romeo—a deeper level of trust and respect that seemed to fill the room like an invisible thread weaving us all together. It was palpable, almost tangible, wrapping around us in a cocoon of shared understanding.

"Our previous chef suffered an injury and won't be back for six months," Romeo explained, his tone softened by genuine concern. "I didn't want you to stress yourself cooking for me while running your business, amore. I want your success always." The sincerity in his voice wrapped around me like a warm embrace, igniting a surge of love and appreciation for his thoughtfulness.

As the conversation flowed, I couldn't help but notice the way Romeo's eyes gleamed with a quiet intensity whenever he mentioned Luca's name. It was as if there was an unspoken understanding between them, a bond that transcended the typical employer-employee dynamic.

Caroline, too, seemed to sense it; her expression subtly shifted, hinting that she was privy to some secret that existed between the two men—a hidden world that I wasn't yet a part of.

As lunch came to a close, Romeo leaned back in his chair, his gaze never leaving mine, the air between us thick with unspoken affection. "I'm glad you're comfortable with Caroline," he said, his voice low and husky, wrapping me in a blanket of warmth that made everything else fade away. "She's been a valuable addition to our household."

I smiled, my heart swelling with gratitude. "I can see that. Thank you for thinking of me." My words were sincere, reflecting the deep bond we shared, one built on trust and mutual support.

His gaze bore into my soul, intense and unwavering. "I always think of you, amore. You are my priority." The warmth of his connection enveloped me, filling the spaces of doubt with certainty and strength.

Just then, Caroline's eyes lit up with enthusiasm as she spoke passionately about her love for old movies. "I adore classic films!" she exclaimed, her eyes sparkling like stars in the night sky. "There's something about the dialogue, the drama... ' like a warm cup of tea on a rainy day." Her voice was melodic, each word laced with nostalgia and fondness.

My heart skipped a beat, and an unsettling memory flashed through my mind, vivid and intrusive. "Jamie used to say that same thing!" I whispered, my voice barely audible, a tremor betraying my emotional state. The name hung in the air, heavy with unspoken history and echoes of past pain.

Caroline's smile faltered for a brief moment, her composure slipping like a delicate thread unraveling. But she quickly regained it, her voice light and airy. "What a wonderful coincidence!" she said, though I could sense an undercurrent of tension swirling around her words, a ripple of discomfort that hinted at something deeper beneath the surface.

Romeo's eyes narrowed, darting between us like a hawk sensing prey. "Caroline, tell us more about your love for old movies," he urged, his voice low and smooth, as if coaxing a hidden truth from her. There was an intensity in his gaze, a desire to uncover layers that remained concealed.

As Caroline launched into a passionate discussion about Hitchcock and Hepburn, her hands animatedly illustrating her points, I couldn't shake the feeling that she knew more about Jamie than she let on. The similarities in their words and passions felt like fragments of a puzzle, each piece hinting at a larger picture just beyond my grasp—an image I was desperate to see clearly.

The evening wore on, and our conversation flowed like a gentle stream until Caroline's phone pierced the air, shrill and insistent. She hesitated, her eyes darting toward Romeo, a flicker of uncertainty passing over her features before she rose from her seat, her movements fluid and graceful.

"Excuse me for a moment," she said, her voice low and mysterious, as she glided toward the French doors, her phone pressed to her ear. The soft click of the door closing behind her felt like a barrier separating us from the outside world.

I watched, curiosity piqued, as Caroline stepped into the moonlit garden, her voice hushed and urgent. The laughter and music from inside faded, replaced by the soft rustle of leaves and Caroline's muffled tones, creating an air of secrecy that made my heart race and my mind whirl with questions.

Romeo's gaze followed Caroline, his expression unreadable, before he turned to me, his eyes gleaming with intrigue. "She's a private person," he said, his voice low and smooth, carrying an air of unspoken admiration. "But she's loyal once you've earned her trust." His words hung in the air, heavy with meaning, making me wonder just how well he knew her and what secrets lay buried in the depths of her heart.

I nodded, my mind racing with questions as Caroline returned, her face a mask of serenity, yet her eyes betrayed a flicker of unease that sent a shiver down my spine. There was something in her demeanor that felt off, a shadow that lurked just beneath the surface.

"Everything okay?" I asked gently, concern lacing my words like the delicate threads of a tapestry. My instincts urged me to dig deeper, to unearth the truth hidden beneath layers of charm and composure.

Caroline's smile was a fraction too bright, her laughter a shade too forced. "Just a wrong number," she said, her eyes darting toward Romeo before she turned back to me. "Where were we? Ah yes, old movies..."

But the spell was broken, the atmosphere subtly shifting like a shadow cast across the room. My suspicions were aroused, and my mind raced with possibilities as I wondered what secrets Caroline might be hiding. Did she share a past with Jamie that I was unaware of? The notion unsettled me, creating a pit of uncertainty in my stomach.

I pushed the thoughts aside, reluctant to jump to conclusions, but the feeling lingered like a whisper in the back of my mind, tugging at my curiosity and compelling me to explore the depths of Caroline's story.

As we continued talking, I couldn't shake the sense that there was more to Caroline than met the eye. The polished exterior she presented felt like a façade, a carefully crafted image that concealed the complexities of her life. I found myself wondering what lay beneath, hidden in the depths of her enigmatic smile and bright laughter.

CHAPTER THIRTY

MIA BIANCHI

I stepped out of the luxury hotel, the golden sunlight pouring over me like a warm embrace, stirring a rush of relief, excitement, and a flutter of fear in my chest. The air was filled with the tantalizing scent of blooming jasmine, a fragrant promise of the day ahead. As I turned to find Romeo, he was already there, waiting for me with an intensity in his gaze that made my heart race. He took my hand, his grip warm and reassuring, grounding me in the moment.

"Mia, posso chiederti qualcosa?" he asked, his voice low and husky, wrapping around me like a soft caress, drawing me closer to him.

"Of course, amore," I replied, tilting my head back to meet his eyes, a smile blossoming on my lips as anticipation danced in my chest.

"What do you love most about me?" he inquired, his eyes sparkling with curiosity, a hint of vulnerability flickering beneath the surface.

I paused, my mind racing with all the things I adored about Romeo. His passion, his kindness, the way he seemed to understand me in ways no one else did. "I love your passion," I said finally, choosing my words with care, wanting to convey the depth of my feelings. "The way you throw yourself into everything you do, with such intensity and conviction. It's captivating."

A radiant smile spread across Romeo's face, his eyes sparkling with warmth that melted the lingering edges of my fear. "Io amo la tua gentilezza," he replied, his voice thick with emotion, echoing the sincerity in my heart that surged in response.

We continued walking, the world around us bustling with life yet fading into a comforting blur as the silence between us felt like a cherished secret. The sun hung high in the sky, casting a golden hue over everything, and the warmth seeped into my skin, making me feel alive.

Then, Romeo stopped suddenly, turning to face me, his excitement palpable as he shared, "Mia, voglio portarti in un posto speciale." His eyes gleamed with anticipation, making my stomach flutter with excitement.

Before long, we arrived at a stunning villa on the outskirts of town, its grandeur taking my breath away. The building stood proudly amid lush gardens, with vibrant flowers spilling over the pathways and a tranquil lake that glimmered like a thousand diamonds under the sun. As we walked inside, I was greeted by the sight of a sumptuous feast awaiting us, the table adorned with delicate linens and flickering candles casting a warm, inviting glow over the room. Soft music floated through the air, wrapping around us like a cozy blanket, setting the perfect ambiance for an unforgettable evening.

"Mia, questo è incredibile," I breathed, my eyes wide with wonder as I took in the beauty surrounding me.

Romeo's smile widened, pride glowing in his eyes. "Volevo darti una notte da ricordare," he said, his voice thick with emotion, making my heart swell with love and appreciation.

As the evening unfolded, we strolled through the gardens hand in hand, the stars twinkling above us like a million tiny lanterns. The air was fragrant with the sweet scent of blooming flowers, and the gentle sound of crickets serenaded us, creating a soothing backdrop that made the moment feel magical.

"Mia, ho qualcosa da mostrarti," Romeo said, his voice low and mysterious, drawing me in closer, as if sharing a secret meant just for us.

He led me to a secluded spot, where a beautiful fountain bubbled and splashed, its waters dancing in the moonlight. In the center stood a stunning statue of a woman, her face serene and peaceful, capturing the essence of beauty in a timeless moment. The moonlight cast a soft glow on the statue, making it appear almost ethereal.

"Chi è?" I asked, my voice barely above a whisper, captivated by the elegance of the sculpture.

Romeo smiled, his eyes shining with love and tenderness. "Sei tu, Mia."

Tears pricked at the corners of my eyes as I gazed at the statue, overwhelmed by emotion. This was the most romantic night of my life, a moment I knew I would carry with me forever, a treasure etched into my heart.

But as we walked back toward the villa, the serene magic of the evening began to shift ever so slightly. The air, once warm and inviting, now felt heavy, and a subtle tension seemed to hang between us. Romeo's grip on my hand tightened imperceptibly, and the weight of the moment shifted.

As we entered the villa, the atmosphere thickened in a way that I couldn't quite place. Romeo's expression hardened as he opened the door to his bedroom, revealing Caroline standing over my bed, her hands hovering above my face in a moment of shock. The air thickened with tension.

"Caroline, cosa stai facendo?" he demanded, his voice low and even, filled with an intensity that sent chills racing down my spine.

Caroline let out a startled yelp, her eyes wide with fear. "Romeo, io... io stavo solo controllando Mia," she stammered, her voice trembling, betraying her unease.

Romeo's gaze remained locked on Caroline, narrowing as suspicion clouded his features. "A mezzanotte? Senza svegliarmi?" he pressed, his tone sharp, thick with gravity.

Caroline took a step back, her eyes darting toward the door, searching for an escape. "Io... io non volevo disturbarti," she said, her voice barely above a whisper, laced with guilt.

Romeo's eyes narrowed further, determination etched into his expression. "Caroline, cosa stai nascondendo?"

But Caroline only looked scared and embarrassed, her bravado crumbling under his scrutiny. She took another hesitant step back, the tremor in her voice evident.

He sighed, his shoulders relaxing slightly, though his concern remained palpable. "Caroline, apprezzo la tua preoccupazione, ma per favore rispetta la nostra privacy. Se Mia ha bisogno di qualcosa, mi occuperò io."

Caroline nodded hastily, her eyes downcast, an expression of shame washing over her features. "Sì, sir. Mi dispiace, sir." She quickly scurried out of the room, leaving Romeo with a whirlwind of thoughts swirling in his mind.

He shook his head, chuckling wryly, but the nagging feeling of unease lingered like a shadow in the back of his mind. Caroline was a great cook, but sometimes her enthusiasm seemed to tiptoe over the line of propriety. Still, the deeper sense of discomfort gnawed at him. Something wasn't right.

In the following days, Romeo summoned his head of security, Marco, his brow furrowed with concern. "Marco, I need you to investigate Caroline," he instructed, his voice low and serious. "I want to know everything about her. Where she came from, who she is... everything."

"On it, boss," Marco replied, his expression grave, understanding the weight of the task at hand.

Days turned into weeks, yet Marco returned empty-handed, the look on his face conveying his frustration. "Caroline's a ghost, boss," he said with a shrug. "No one knows anything about her past. It's like she just appeared out of nowhere."

Romeo's eyes narrowed, his mind racing with the implications. What was Caroline hiding? It didn't sit well with him, and he decided to confront her directly. But when he arrived in the kitchen, she was nowhere to be found.

"Dov'è Caroline?" he demanded, his voice echoing through the halls, a sense of urgency rising within him.

The staff exchanged nervous glances, their unease palpable. "Non l'abbiamo vista, sir," one stammered, their eyes darting anxiously.

Romeo's face darkened, fists clenching in frustration. Where had Caroline gone? The trust he had placed in her felt foolish now, a blind spot in his judgment.

"Marco!" he bellowed. "Raddoppia la sicurezza! Voglio occhi e orecchie ovunque!"

"Già fatto, boss," Marco replied, moving quickly to follow orders, determination etched on his face.

Romeo began to pace, his mind racing with unanswered questions. What had Caroline been planning? Where was she now? His instincts told him something was off, but he couldn't put his finger on it.

As the sun dipped below the horizon, an unsettling silence settled over the villa. The warmth of our earlier moments felt distant, replaced by an undercurrent of tension that made my heart race. I sensed Romeo's unease radiating from him, an energy that was almost tangible. In an attempt to soothe the storm brewing within him, I reached for his hand, hoping to provide comfort amidst the uncertainty.

"Mia, I need you to trust me," he said, his voice steady but laced with concern. "I'm going to get to the bottom of this. Whatever it takes."

"Whatever it takes, Romeo. I believe in you," I said, squeezing his hand tightly, determination mingling with the fear swirling inside me.

The night stretched on, filled with uncertainty and shadows that loomed just beyond our grasp. Yet amidst the darkness, I found solace in the strength of our bond, the warmth of his presence reminding me that we were in this together, even as secrets threatened to unravel the happiness we had only just begun to build.

CHAPTER THIRTY-ONE

MIA BIANCHI

As I settled into the plush leather seat of the Bentley, a thrill of excitement coursed through me, wrapping around my heart like a warm embrace. The familiar scent of polished wood and luxury leather filled the air, mingling with the soft hum of the engine. Romeo slid in beside me, his presence igniting a spark that sent shivers down my spine. His eyes locked onto mine, radiating an intensity that made my pulse quicken.

"Bella mia," he whispered, his Italian accent weaving through the air like a melody, setting my heart aflame. The chauffeur closed the door behind us, sealing us away from the outside world, and the soft click of the lock felt like a promise of secrecy.

I could feel the heat of Romeo's body so close to mine. Our hands brushed together, a fleeting touch that ignited a rush of warmth. I didn't pull away; instead, I welcomed his touch, letting our fingers intertwine like vines in a garden, creating an unbreakable bond.

As we glided through the night streets, the city lights blurred into a kaleidoscope of color, painting the windows with a vibrant glow. I lost myself in Romeo's gaze, which burned with a desire that mirrored my own. The air was thick with anticipation, mingling the scent of luxury leather with the sweet fragrance of my perfume, creating an intoxicating atmosphere that enveloped us.

His gaze traced the contours of my face, lingering on my lips, causing my breath to hitch in my throat. I could feel his thumb begin to trace soft circles on my palm, sending shivers cascading down my spine, igniting every nerve ending within me.

"Ti desidero," he whispered, his voice low and husky, wrapping around my senses like a silken thread. I could feel the weight of his words, each syllable drenched in an intoxicating mix of desire and vulnerability that made my heart race.

The soundproofing of the car shielded us from the outside world, adding to the thrill of our shared moment. The speed of the Bentley matched the racing of my heart as I melted under his intense stare, becoming one with him in a way that was both exhilarating and terrifying.

Without a word, Romeo pressed a button, and the privacy screen slid up, cocooning us in our world. His eyes devoured me, consuming every inch of my skin, every curve of my face, every beat of my heart. I felt like a feast laid before him, ready to be indulged. The intensity of his gaze left me breathless, a craving building within me that demanded to be satisfied.

Caught up in the moment, I felt a rush of heat between us. Without hesitation, Romeo unfastened his slacks and pulled out his cock, his eyes never leaving mine.

He began to stroke himself, a smirk crossing his face as he watched my reaction. I whimpered, my desire mounting, wanting him to fill me completely. As he continued, pre-come glistened at his tip, and I arched my back, licking my lips as pleasure coursed through me.

When he was on the verge of release, he gestured for me to come closer.

Eagerly, I knelt before him, ready to receive his essence. As he came, his hot, sweet release splattered across my face, and I wasted no time in licking him clean, tasting the essence of his desire.

Without undressing myself, I rose, sliding onto him as he filled me. My nipples hardened at his touch as he gripped my ass, pistoning in and out of me with fervor. The car's interior was filled with the sounds of our passion, every thrust pushing us closer to the edge, creating a symphony of pleasure that resonated deep within my core.

After what felt like both an eternity and a fleeting moment, Romeo roared as he released himself deep within me, holding my shoulders as he pulled me closer. When it was over, he tenderly cleaned me up with wipes from the car, his gentle touch a soothing balm to my flushed skin.

Grateful for his thoughtfulness, I quickly reapplied my makeup, attempting to mask the evidence of our passionate encounter, though the memory lingered like a sweet ache. We arrived at our destination, and with a shared sense of purpose, we dove into our work, though the tension between us remained, a tantalizing undercurrent that threatened to derail our focus.

After a long day filled with meetings and decisions, we finally sat down to a quiet dinner together in a dimly lit restaurant, the atmosphere enveloping us in a sense of intimacy. The flickering candles cast dancing shadows across our faces, allowing us to savor the calm before the storm. Suddenly, the TV in the corner caught our attention, the news anchor's voice slicing through the ambiance.

"...Breaking News: An unidentified body was found earlier today, and authorities have confirmed the victim as Caroline Grey, a resident. The investigation is ongoing, but sources suggest foul play may be involved."

Romeo's eyes widened in disbelief, shock etched across his face as his fork clattered onto the plate. I instinctively covered my mouth, horror flooding my senses.

"No... non può essere," he whispered, his disbelief heavy in the air, his voice barely audible over the murmurs of the surrounding diners.

Tears filled my eyes as I reached for his hand, the connection between us grounding me.

"I'm so sorry, Romeo. This is devastating."

As the news anchor continued, "Sources close to the investigation reveal that Caroline's death may be linked to Jamie's mysterious disappearance, potentially tied to you and protecting you," Romeo's expression darkened, his eyes blazing with a mix of grief and determination.

"Che cosa? Jamie? No... Non posso crederlo," he said, his voice rising with anger, frustration bubbling beneath the surface.

I tightened my grip on his hand, sensing the storm within him.

Romeo's memories flooded back—Caroline, their loyal cook, who had stepped in after Maria's injury. Her warm smile and kindness felt like a ghost in the room, haunting him. "Era più di una cuoca, Mia. She was family," he murmured, his voice tinged with sorrow, each word wrapped in a shroud of loss.

We sat in stunned silence as the news anchor urged anyone with information to come forward, the air growing heavy with grief and resolve. Romeo's gaze drifted toward the kitchen, where Caroline's presence felt palpable, a lingering spirit woven into the fabric of their lives. He had to uncover the truth behind her tragic death.

Without a word, he stood and strode to the security room, urgency in his movements, the world around him fading as he focused on the task at hand.

"Raddoppia la sicurezza intorno a Mia, effective immediately," he ordered Marco, his voice low and fierce, commanding respect and obedience. "I want surveillance equipment in every corner of this mansion. Non voglio nessun punto cieco."

"Consider it done, sir," Marco replied, his expression grim, acknowledging the gravity of the situation.

I approached Romeo, my voice steady yet filled with concern.

"I know you're trying to protect me, but I don't need extra guards. Leo will keep me safe."

His brow furrowed, doubt clouding his features. "Ti fidi di lui così tanto? Do you trust him that much?"

"Yes, I do. It's time we trusted him completely. Send the others away. I'll be fine with just Leo."

Uncertainty flickered in his eyes, but he nodded, his protective instincts at war with my conviction, each heartbeat a reminder of the dangers lurking in the shadows.

"Okay, Mia," he finally conceded, the tension in his shoulders easing slightly. "Manderò via gli altri bodyguards. But if anything happens to you..."

"Nothing will happen, I promise. Jamie will keep me safe."

With a heavy sigh, Romeo turned to Marco. Inform the other bodyguards that their services are no longer needed. Jamie sarà l'unico a proteggere Mia da ora in poi."

As Marco nodded and left, a sense of relief washed over me, intertwining with the tension that had been building since Caroline's news broke. I knew trusting Jamie was the right decision, but my heart ached for the loss that surrounded us.

The next day, as I walked home from the market with Leo, my bodyguard, the sun bathed everything in a golden glow, casting long shadows on the cobblestone streets. A sense of ease enveloped me as we laughed and chatted, enjoying the simple moment, our camaraderie a welcome distraction.

Suddenly, a black van screeched to a halt beside us, the tires squealing against the pavement. My stomach dropped as four masked men jumped out, surrounding us like wolves closing in on their prey.

"Get down!" one yelled, pointing a gun at me, his eyes glinting with malice.

Before I could react, Leo instinctively pushed me behind him, his body a shield against the imminent danger.

"Run, Mia!" he shouted, urgency lacing his words, his body tensed and ready to protect me at all costs.

Fear froze me in place as the gunman took a menacing step closer, his intentions clear.

"You think you can protect her, Leo?" he taunted, a cruel smile spreading across his face, as if to savor the power he wielded in that moment.

"I'll always protect her," Leo replied, determination flooding his voice, a promise of loyalty that filled the air between us.

Then the gunman pulled the trigger, the sound echoing like a thunderclap in my ears. Time seemed to stretch as the world around me blurred, a cacophony of shouts and chaos erupting in slow motion. Leo lunged toward me, his body moving with a fierce determination to shield me, and I felt the adrenaline surge through my veins.

In that instant, I was acutely aware of every heartbeat, every breath, and the intense resolve etched across Leo's face. The bullet whizzed past us, narrowly missing its mark, and the gunman's expression shifted from arrogance to shock. I was frozen in fear, but instinct kicked in, and I grasped Leo's arm tightly, as if my grip alone could anchor us to safety.

"Go!" Leo yelled, his voice cutting through the haze of panic. He pushed me hard, urging me to run. I stumbled back, my heart pounding in my chest, but my legs felt like lead.

"Run, Mia! Don't look back!"

As if the world had shifted back into normal speed, I snapped into action, sprinting down the street, my breaths coming in quick gasps. The sound of shouting and the pounding footsteps behind me ignited a primal fear, propelling me forward.

I could hear Leo fighting behind me, his voice raised in defiance, but I dared not glance back. I needed to escape, to find safety. The adrenaline coursed through me, pushing me past the panic that threatened to consume me. I turned the corner, my feet pounding against the cobblestones, weaving through alleyways as the adrenaline sharpened my senses.

Each footfall echoed my desperation as I sprinted toward the nearest cafe, my sanctuary amidst the chaos. Bursting through the door, I barely noticed the startled patrons as I rushed inside, desperation clawing at my insides.

"Call the police!" I shouted, my voice rising above the clamor.

The barista's eyes widened, and in that moment, I caught a glimpse of my reflection in the glass—the wildness in my eyes and the panic etched across my face was unrecognizable.

"Where's Leo?" I gasped, my heart aching with worry as I fought to regain my composure.

The barista hesitated, but the urgency in my voice seemed to snap him into action. "I'll call! Just stay here!"

I turned, scanning the street through the glass door, my breath hitching as I searched for any sign of Leo. My heart raced, pounding against my ribs, a desperate drumbeat echoing in my ears.

Moments stretched into an eternity, and just when I felt the walls closing in, I spotted him—running toward the cafe, his expression a mix of relief and urgency.

"Get inside!" he shouted, urging me with a fierce wave of his hand as he darted through the doorway.

The moment he stepped in, the tension in my chest began to ease. I rushed to him, my heart soaring as I wrapped my arms around his waist, pulling him close. "I was so scared!" I murmured against his chest, feeling the steady rhythm of his heartbeat beneath my cheek.

"I'm here. I've got you," he whispered, his voice a soothing balm against the chaos of the outside world.

As sirens wailed in the distance, we stood together, the weight of the moment settling around us like a heavy fog. I knew then that we had crossed a threshold, the fragile illusion of safety shattered. But in the depths of my fear, a flicker of something else ignited within me—a fierce resolve. I wouldn't let them take my life away from me.

We would fight back together.

CHAPTER THIRTY-TWO

MIA BIANCHI

As Jamie held me close, the weight of his obsession pressed down on me like a suffocating blanket, smothering me with a cold, familiar fear. His body heat radiated against mine, suffocating me as much as his words. The flickering light above cast distorted shadows that danced eerily across the rough stone walls, amplifying my sense of entrapment and confusion.

I fought against the rising panic, my breath shallow, my pulse racing. My mind was frantic, desperately scrambling for a plan—any way to escape this suffocating reality.

"Jamie," I said, forcing a tremor into my voice, my heart hammering like a trapped bird against my ribs. "I'm so scared. I don't know what's happening to us."

His grip tightened like a vice, the heat of his body pressing into mine, smothering me as he leaned in, his breath brushing my ear with an intensity that made my skin crawl.

"You don't have to be scared, Mia. I'm here to protect you. I love you, remember?" His words dripped with a sincerity that sent a chill down my spine, both reassuring and chilling.

"Love..." The word tasted bitter on my tongue, like ash mingled with regret. "But why all this? Why keep me here?" My voice trembled, a mix of fear and defiance bubbling to the surface, fighting for control.

I struggled to maintain my composure, playing the role of the frightened captive even as my heart thundered in my chest.

"Can't we just go back to how things were? Before all of this?" My eyes searched his, desperate to find a flicker of the Jamie I once knew.

He pulled back slightly, his eyes narrowing, calculating. He weighed my plea against the chaos inside him, and for a moment, I dared to hope. But then his eyes hardened, and his voice dropped into something colder.

"You think I wanted this? You think I wanted to hide you away?" His voice was filled with passion, but it was tinged with desperation. "No, Mia. You don't understand. This is necessary. You're the light, and I'm the darkness that surrounds you. I'm doing this for your good."

"You're good?" I repeated, letting disbelief flood my tone. "This isn't love, Jamie! This is madness!" The words escaped before I could stop them, the raw frustration and sorrow spilling over, threatening to drown me in its tide.

His face twisted, a storm of anger and anguish flashing across his features, an unsettling mix of passion and pain that unsettled me further.

"Madness? You think you know what madness is? You have no idea what I've sacrificed for you, what I've done to keep you safe!" His voice rose, bouncing off the cold stone walls, reverberating with the madness inside him.

I took a deep breath, steadying myself as I chose my words carefully. "Then let me help you. If you love me, let's get out of here. I don't want to be a prisoner anymore."

A flicker of uncertainty crossed his eyes, and for a moment, I thought I saw a crack in his facade. But just as quickly, that glimmer of softness hardened again, replaced by an unyielding resolve.

"You think you can manipulate me, Mia? You're smarter than I thought. But I'm not falling for it." His tone became resolute, the walls closing in between us once again.

As he spoke, my gaze caught something metallic on the bedside table—a small knife, likely for cutting ropes or, more ominously, for threatening me further. My heart raced at the sight. A dangerous thrill coursed through me. Could this be the opportunity I'd been waiting for? I knew I couldn't act yet, not with him so close, but the thought of defending myself gave me a sliver of hope. I had to bide my time, keep him talking, gather my strength.

"Please, Jamie. I'm begging you," I whispered, lowering my voice to a soft plea, desperation coloring my tone. "I don't want to be afraid of you. I want to understand. Let's just talk. I promise I'll listen."

He hesitated, his breath quickening, the internal struggle evident in the shifting storm of his expression. "You don't understand, Mia. I'm doing this because I have to. Because I can't lose you."

"Then prove it. Prove that you love me. Let's leave this place together," I urged, my voice softening, wrapping around him like a warm embrace, hoping to coax out the man I once loved. "I can't bear this anymore."

For a fleeting moment, I thought I saw a crack in his facade. A glimmer of the Jamie I once knew, a tenderness buried beneath the darkness that had consumed him. But just as quickly, that resolve hardened again, the cold steel of his determination returning.

"No," he said firmly, his eyes piercing mine with finality. "You're safer here. This is where you belong."

Despair clawed at my insides, an unrelenting creature gnawing at my resolve. But I forced a smile, hiding the panic that threatened to consume me. "Okay, if that's what you believe... I'll stay."

His eyes softened, a flicker of approval lighting them. He pulled me into another embrace, his body warm yet suffocating against mine.

"Good girl," he whispered, his breath tickling my ear, sending a fresh shiver of unease down my spine. "You'll see. Everything will be alright."

But as I lay there in his arms, a plan began to form in my mind, slowly weaving its way through the fog of my fear. I needed to create an opportunity—one where I could use that knife, where I could fight back. For now, I would play the part, but I wouldn't give up. Not now. Not ever.

Then, something struck me, a sudden revelation that crashed over me like a wave breaking against the shore. Jamie's voice had changed over time. There was something more polished, more controlled in his tone than I remembered. It unsettled me, like a subtle shift that felt wrong.

It wasn't just the voice. His features were different, too. Sharper, more defined. His expressions felt unfamiliar, almost alien. The realization hit me like a sledgehammer: Jamie had undergone surgery.

Leo. The bodyguard Romeo had hired to protect me... could it be? My heart raced as I pieced it together. Leo wasn't just Jamie's alias—Jamie had undergone surgery to become Leo. He had been hiding in plain sight this entire time, manipulating everything around me while I remained blissfully unaware.

The truth was sickening. A bitter pill lodged in my throat, a jagged shard of betrayal that cut deep. My mind spun as I looked at the man holding me captive. This wasn't just my toxic ex-boyfriend. Jamie had transformed into Leo, weaving himself back into my life, lurking in the shadows while playing the role of protector.

"Jamie," I whispered, unable to mask the shock in my voice, my words barely a breath against the weight of my discovery.

He stiffened at the sound of his real name, his grip tightening around me, the tension crackling in the air like electricity. His eyes—the one thing surgery couldn't change—flickered with recognition, a flash of acknowledgment that sent a chill down my spine. He knew that I had uncovered his secret.

His voice dropped to a chilling whisper, laced with a possessive edge that sent shivers down my spine. "Now you understand, Mia. I never left you. I've always been by your side."

CHAPTER THIRTY-THREE

ROMEO GIUSEPPE

My heart pounded like a war drum as I drove through the city's darkened streets, a chaotic swirl of fear and frustration clouding my thoughts. The weight of uncertainty pressed down on me like a vise, suffocating every breath. "Dove sei, Mia? Dove sei?" I whispered under my breath in Italian, each word thick with mounting desperation, reverberating in the stillness of the night.

I had searched every place I could think of—her favorite cafes, those cherished spots where laughter once flowed freely, even her workplace where the aroma of fresh coffee mingled with the chatter of her colleagues—but Mia was nowhere to be found. It felt as though she had vanished from the face of the earth, leaving behind only the echo of her vibrant presence that deepened my despair. The air around me thickened with dread, a suffocating shroud that made it hard to breathe, and I could sense the walls closing in, constricting my chest.

The realization hit me like a punch to the gut: Jamie wasn't just some ex-boyfriend from Mia's past; he was a monster, a calculated predator, lying in wait, lurking in the shadows of her life. My heart sank as I understood the true depth of the danger she was in. How had I been so blind to the storm brewing beneath the surface?

As I pulled up to my apartment, it now felt like a hollow shell of the sanctuary it once was. The warmth and security I had taken for granted crumbled around me like the walls of a fortress under siege, leaving me exposed, vulnerable. I had lost everything—my home, my sense of safety, and the woman I loved.

Desperation drove me to extreme measures. I hired a dozen hackers to track Mia's location. It was a gamble, a risky play fueled by my unwavering need to find her, needed to save her from whatever nightmare Jamie had in store.

The call from the hackers sliced through my panic like a blade. "Romeo, we've found her. She's at an abandoned hospital on the outskirts. There's a decoy ambulance outside—don't be fooled. It's a trap."

My blood ran cold, a chill settling deep in my bones. "Grazie," I replied, my voice tight with fear and determination. "I'm on my way."

As I drove toward the hospital, I fought to steady my racing thoughts, pushing back the tide of panic threatening to consume me. The building loomed ahead, its silhouette jagged against the dark sky, an ominous reminder of the horror that could be inside. I parked a safe distance away, my eyes scanning the scene, alert for any sign of movement. The ambulance outside was too obvious, a blatant lure, a bait designed to ensnare anyone who dared approach.

My heart raced as I approached the building, each step echoing my growing anxiety in the stillness of the night. "Mia, dove sei?" I whispered, my voice trembling with fear and hope as I pushed open the creaky doors. The musty smell of decay and abandonment hit me like a physical blow, a stark contrast to the vibrant life that should have filled this place with warmth and laughter.

Silence wrapped around me, oppressive and thick, broken only by the sound of my breath and the distant echoes of my footsteps reverberating through the hollow hallways. Following a faint noise—a whimper that pierced through the stillness—I ventured deeper into the hospital's labyrinthine corridors, each turn amplifying my dread.

When I reached an old operating room, my heart dropped into my stomach. It was empty. Panic surged through me like wildfire as I rushed to check the nearby rooms, my mind racing with terrifying possibilities. "Mia!" I shouted, my voice slicing through the silence, but all that answered me was the echo of my voice, mocking my desperation.

Despair settled like a heavy cloak over my shoulders as I searched room after room, my hopes dwindling with each passing moment. Where could she be? I couldn't bear the thought of Jamie having her, his grasp tightening around her. Just as I was about to lose hope completely, I heard a voice—a soft, muffled sound coming from down the hall.

"Mia?" I called out, urgency fueling my steps. I followed the sound, my heart racing, praying it was her. But when I burst into the next room, it was just more darkness and decay, the flickering lights above casting eerie shadows across the walls, like ghosts of the past haunting this forsaken place.

Desperation clawed at my insides. I pulled out my phone to call her, but it went straight to voicemail—a grim reminder of my isolation. My breath quickened, panic rising in my chest. "No...no, this can't be happening," I whispered, feeling like I was spiraling into madness, the walls closing in around me.

Backing out of the room, frustration boiled over. I had to find her. I would not leave this place without her, no matter the cost.

After what felt like hours of searching, I finally stumbled upon an old storage closet. Yanking the door open, I peered inside—empty, a black hole of despair. But as I turned to leave, a chilling realization hit me: Jamie could be close.

I stepped back, adrenaline coursing through my veins like ice. I had to get out of here. Just as I turned, I heard a noise—a faint scraping sound echoing from the operating room. My heart stopped, and I rushed back, hope and fear battling within me.

"Mia!" I shouted again, my voice a desperate plea, hoping against hope that she could hear me. But there was nothing, only the oppressive silence of the abandoned building pressing in around me.

Frustration morphed into panic, an insidious whisper in my mind that I was running out of time. I had to find her before it was too late, before the shadows consumed her.

"Mia, where are you?" I muttered, my voice barely a whisper, trembling with fear. "Please, just give me a sign."

But there was nothing. I took a deep breath, forcing myself to stay calm, to push back against the encroaching despair, and prepared to search the building again. I would find her, no matter what it took, no matter how dark the path ahead seemed.

CHAPTER THIRTY- FOUR

MIA BIANCHI

I tried to escape, but every attempt felt futile, like invisible chains tethered me to this hell. Days bled into nights in the dank, abandoned hospital where Jamie—no, Leo, the monster I had never truly seen—kept me captive. Each moment stretched painfully, like an endless nightmare that showed no sign of release. He thrived on my suffering, feeding off the torment in my eyes, his jealousy burning bright, fueled by a betrayal he couldn't forgive.

"You always had your eyes on Romeo, you fucking liar!" His voice lashed out like a whip, sharp and cutting, dripping with venomous contempt. The dim light from the window cast shadows across his face, distorting his features, making him look even more menacing.

I trembled beneath his piercing gaze, my heart racing in terror. My voice cracked as I whimpered, "Please, Jamie, you have to believe me—I never meant for this to happen."

But my words fell like ashes between us, dissolving in the cold, merciless air.

His eyes narrowed, blazing with fury. "I'll teach you what happens when you betray me," he snarled, his voice low but laced with an ominous promise.

Before I could respond, his hands seized my legs with an iron grip, his fingers digging into my skin with brutal force. He yanked me across the filthy, bloodstained floor, the grime coating my clothes, the rough tiles scraping against my bare skin, leaving raw marks in their wake. My body was dragged like a lifeless doll, powerless beneath his merciless rage.

"Please!" I cried out, my voice hoarse with desperation. "I'm sorry!" My sobs echoed through the desolate hospital corridors, but they only seemed to fuel his anger.

Jamie's face twisted into a sadistic grin as he loomed over me, his breath hot against my face. "You think sorry is going to fix this?" His voice was a low growl, vibrating with madness. "You gave yourself to Romeo. You let him touch you, didn't you? Did he make you feel special? Better than I ever could?"

The accusation hit me like a punch, and my chest tightened with guilt and fear. "Jamie, I swear, I never wanted to hurt you," I whispered, my voice faltering. "I didn't mean for any of this—"

"Shut up!" he roared, his voice reverberating through the space, sending chills down my spine. His hand shot out, gripping my chin painfully tight, forcing me to look into his cold, rage-filled eyes. "I was the one who loved you! I was the one who promised you everything, and this is how you repay me?"

A sob escaped my lips as his words cut deeper than any physical wound ever could. He released my chin with a harsh shove, his lips curling into a twisted smirk as he kicked me in the stomach with brutal force. The impact stole the breath from my lungs, and I curled in on myself, gasping as pain radiated through my entire body.

"Did you scream for him like you're screaming now?" he sneered, kicking me again. "Did he hear you beg?"

"I didn't—" I gasped, tears streaming down my face, my chest heaving. "It wasn't like that... I—"

But my words were swallowed by another wave of pain as Jamie grabbed a fistful of my hair and dragged me further across the cold, unforgiving floor. My scalp burned, and my vision blurred as he yanked me forward with savage strength, my body too weak to resist.

"Shut up!" His voice was savage, unforgiving. "You think I care about your excuses?" He shoved my face into the dirt and grime of the floor, pressing my cheek against the cold, filthy tiles. I tasted the bitter tang of blood and dust, my spirit crumbling under the weight of his relentless cruelty.

"Please, Jamie..." My voice cracked, barely more than a whisper. "I'm sorry. I never wanted this."

"Stupid, lying whore!" he screamed, his voice ringing with pure hatred. He spat on me, the warm droplets mixing with the cold filth beneath me. "You deserve everything you're getting."

He finally let go of me, his grip releasing my hair as he stormed out of the room, slamming the door with such force that it reverberated through the walls. The silence that followed was suffocating, broken only by the sound of my ragged breathing. I lay there in a heap, too weak to move, too broken to think.

Time passed in a blur. I didn't know how long I lay there, my body aching, my mind a haze of fear and exhaustion. I wanted to sleep, but my thoughts wouldn't stop racing, every creak of the building making me flinch, terrified he would return.

When the door creaked open again, it was morning. Jamie—or Leo—stood in the doorway, silhouetted by the light streaming in behind him. I could barely move, my muscles weak from dehydration and fatigue. My lips were cracked, my throat dry as sandpaper. Every inch of my body screamed in pain.

He walked toward me slowly, the steady, deliberate tap of his footsteps filling the room with tension. His gaze locked onto mine, cold and unfeeling, as he carried a jug of water in his hands. For a brief, desperate moment, I thought he was going to help me, give me something to drink. But I should have known better.

With a wicked smile, he poured the water over my trembling body. The ice-cold liquid hit me like a shockwave, sending violent shudders through me as I gasped from the sensation. The freezing water drenched me, soaking my clothes and chilling me to the bone. My teeth chattered uncontrollably, my body curling in on itself in a futile attempt to preserve warmth.

"Look at you," Jamie taunted, his voice dripping with malice. "Pathetic. Weak. And you thought you could run from me?" He crouched down, his eyes gleaming with a sick satisfaction as he watched me shiver. "You really thought you were better than me, didn't you?"

Tears filled my eyes again, but I refused to let them fall. Not this time. I wouldn't give him the satisfaction of seeing me cry again.

"You did this to us," he continued, his voice softening into a mockery of affection as he reached out to stroke my wet hair. "You destroyed everything, Mia. If you had just stayed loyal to me, none of this would've happened."

His touch made my skin crawl, but I was too weak to pull away. I lay there, soaked and trembling, feeling like the very life was being drained out of me. But in the deepest, darkest part of me, something stirred. A spark of defiance, a flicker of strength that refused to die.

I had lost so much—my freedom, my dignity, my hope— but I hadn't lost myself. Not yet. He could beat me down, tear me apart, but I wouldn't give him the satisfaction of breaking me completely.

"I'll get out of here," I whispered to myself, my voice barely audible, but the words burned with a newfound resolve.

"I'll escape. And when I do, I'll make him pay for every single thing he's done to me."

Jamie's eyes flickered with amusement as he stood up and looked down at me. "What was that? You got something to say?"

I didn't answer. I just stared up at him, refusing to let him see the fear that still lurked beneath the surface. My silence was my rebellion, my way of telling him that he hadn't won yet.

He narrowed his eyes, as if sensing the shift in me, but after a moment, he snorted and turned away. "You're not going anywhere, Mia. You're mine, now and forever."

As he walked away, the door slamming behind him, I lay in the cold, empty room, my body aching and broken. But my mind—my spirit—was still intact.

I would find a way out. I would survive this nightmare. And one day, I would make sure Jamie—Leo, or whatever name he decided to hide behind, paid for every scar, every tear, every moment of pain he had inflicted on me.

CHAPTER THIRTY- FIVE

MIA BIANCHI

The air in the abandoned hospital was thick and suffocating, saturated with the pungent stench of mold and decay. I lay on the cold, unforgiving floor, bound tightly by ropes that bit into my skin, shivering from the bitter chill and the bruises that marred my body. Every inch of me ached from Jamie's relentless brutality. His cruelty seemed to know no bounds, and the pain of his fists and his words had left me shattered, hollow.

Each passing hour blurred into an eternity, and every second felt like a lifetime of agony. My thoughts spiraled into a chaotic swirl of fear and desperation, gnawing at my will to survive.

A dim light flickered overhead, casting jagged shadows across the crumbling walls, making the once sterile halls of the hospital now seem like a mausoleum of despair. Every breath I took felt labored, each inhale thick with the decay that surrounded me.

The walls seemed to close in on me, pressing down like a vice. Hope was slipping away, yet somewhere deep inside, I clung to the belief that Romeo was searching for me. I had to believe it. If I let go of that hope, I feared I would fall into an abyss I'd never climb out of.

With my eyes closed, I could almost escape, almost convince myself this was a nightmare. Memories of Romeo flooded my mind—the warmth of his smile, the tenderness in his touch. Moments we had shared replayed in my head like flashes of light in the darkness.

It was torture, thinking of how far away those moments felt now, how the laughter and love were now starkly contrasted by the horror I was living. I prayed for death to take me, to free me from this waking nightmare. But something inside me—a flicker of survival—refused to let go.

Suddenly, the silence was broken by the heavy door creaking open. The sound was like a scream in the stillness, and my heart leapt into my throat as fear surged through me. Footsteps echoed ominously in the room, the sound slow and deliberate, approaching me. My body tensed, every nerve on edge. It could only be him. Jamie... no, Leo, the man I no longer recognized.

He strolled into the room like he owned the world, dragging a chair behind him, the scraping sound of its legs against the cracked tiles reverberating through the room, like nails on a chalkboard. The noise was enough to make my skin crawl, and it sent shivers down my spine.

He placed the chair next to me with deliberate care, his movements calculated, confident, like a predator circling its prey. I couldn't look at him. I couldn't face the monster he had become.

"Look at you, Mia," he sneered, his voice dripping with twisted amusement. "Such a mess. Always had a talent for getting into trouble, didn't you?" His tone was casual, almost playful, but there was a venomous edge beneath it.

I flinched at the sound of his voice, trying to shrink into myself. "Please, Jamie," I begged, my voice barely audible, fragile. "Let me go. I don't want this..."

His expression twisted into something dark, sinister. "You think you can just beg your way out of this?" he spat, eyes narrowing as he leaned closer. "You don't get to decide anything anymore. You gave up that right when you betrayed me."

Before I could react, he grabbed a fistful of my hair and yanked my head back, forcing me to look up at him. I winced, biting back the cry of pain that threatened to escape. His eyes bore into mine with a sickening intensity, a deranged glint that sent waves of terror crashing through me.

"I loved you once," he hissed, his grip tightening painfully on my hair. "But that was before you spread your legs for him for Romeo." His voice dripped with venom as he spat the name like it was poison. "I was going to show you what real love felt like, Mia. But now... now I'll show you what true pain is."

Tears welled up in my eyes, but I forced the words out, desperate. "Jamie, no," I whimpered. "I never wanted to hurt you. I loved you... I did love you." My voice cracked, my heart pounding in my chest. Maybe there was still a part of him I could reach—the Jamie I had once known. Maybe I could break through the darkness.

But all I got in return was laughter—a cold, hollow laugh that echoed through the room, void of any warmth or humanity. "Love?" he scoffed, releasing his grip on my hair, letting my head drop back to the floor. "You don't know what love is. But don't worry, Mia," he leaned in again, his breath hot and foul against my skin, "I'm going to teach you. I'll show you how it feels to be destroyed."

A chill ran through me as his words settled like ice in my veins. He wasn't done. He was just getting started. And I didn't know how much more I could endure.

He crouched down beside me, his voice dropping to a dark, ominous whisper. "I killed Caroline, you know," he said casually, like he was talking about the weather. "She thought she could tell you everything.

Thought she could spill my secrets. But I took care of her before she could."

My blood ran cold. Caroline... my friend... died because of him. "No..." I whispered, shaking my head in disbelief. "You didn't..."

"Oh, but I did," he replied, a sick grin spreading across his face. "And I'll do it again. You think you can trust anyone, Mia? You think they'll come to save you? You'll see soon enough where trust gets you."

"You killed her for nothing," I said, my voice shaking with rage. "She was innocent, and you murdered her."

"Innocent?" He scoffed, his grin widening. "She was a traitor. And traitors deserve what they get. Just like you will if you don't learn your place. But you, Mia... you're special. I'm going to make sure you understand that."

I stared at him, my body trembling, trying to hold back the sobs that threatened to tear from my chest. The man I once loved was gone. What stood before me was a monster.

He stood and began pacing the room, his tone shifting again, unsettling in its affection. "You've been a very bad girl, Mia. Always running off to other men, thinking you could escape me." His voice darkened as he continued, "But you were mine. No one else's. I may have slept with others, but you? You were special."

His next confession sent a fresh wave of terror crashing over me. "Those people at the wedding... they weren't even my real parents," he said, a grin spreading across his face.

"Just a couple I paid to play the part. And when did they know too much? I killed them."

I gasped, horrified, my breath coming in short, ragged bursts. He seemed to revel in my fear, his grin widening.

"I've killed women, Mia. So many. For fun, mostly. But I spared Evra—for you. I could've taken her life just like the others, but I didn't. Because you were special."

My voice was barely a whisper as I asked, "Why are you telling me this?"

"Because, Mia," he said, stepping closer, his eyes gleaming with fervor. "I want you to understand how far I'll go for you. I've done everything to keep you safe. I've killed for you. And I'd do it again."

"This isn't love," I breathed, tears streaming down my face. "This is madness."

He leaned down again, his face inches from mine, his breath hot against my skin.

"Madness?" he repeated, his voice cold and low. "You don't even know what madness is. But you will. I'm the only one who truly understands you. The only one who can make you feel alive."

Tears blurred my vision as I shook my head, my voice trembling. "Not like this. I can't love someone who destroys me."

His face twisted in anger, his eyes flashing dangerously. "Love is pain, Mia," he snarled, grabbing my face, forcing me to look at him. "And I'm going to make sure you feel every bit of it."

I shut my eyes, my heart pounding in my chest, terror flooding through me. I needed to escape. I needed to fight. But my body felt weak, broken. All I could do was endure, hoping, praying, that somewhere out there, Romeo was coming.

CHAPTER THIRTY- SIX

MIA BIANCHI

The door creaked open, and Jamie stepped inside, his shadow stretching long across the floor as the faint light from the hallway caught his figure. His form, tall and imposing, seemed to suck the air from the room as a slow, twisted smile curled his lips. My heart sank into my stomach, each beat heavy with dread. I knew what was coming—knew it from the moment his eyes locked onto mine, filled with that all-too-familiar sadistic gleam.

He took his time walking toward me, his steps slow and deliberate, each one sending a chill down my spine. A cigarette dangled from his fingers, the smoke curling lazily in the air between us, but his attention was all on me. "Well, well, if it isn't my stupid little bitch," he sneered, venom in his voice coiling around my throat like an invisible leash. His words stung like a slap to the face, but it was nothing compared to what came next.

Without warning, he brought his foot crashing down on my stomach, hard and vicious. Pain exploded in my abdomen, sharp and blinding, knocking the wind from my lungs. I gasped, my body convulsing as I struggled for air, the world spinning around me in a blur of agony.

"Are you ready to be my obedient girl again?" he taunted, his voice low and cold as he began pacing the room, each step heavy with malice. The sound of his boots against the floor was a chilling reminder of how powerless I was in that moment. His every movement, every word, dripped with cruelty, the kind of cruelty that made you feel small, insignificant—prey trapped in the clutches of a merciless predator.

I fought to hold back the tears threatening to spill from my eyes, clenching my fists tight as if the pain in my hands could distract me from the terror flooding my veins. "Jamie, please... I can't..." My voice cracked, barely a whisper, but the words were out before I could stop them. I hated how weak I sounded, hated how much power he held over me. But even as I spoke, I knew it wouldn't make a difference. He wasn't here to listen.

He laughed, a dark, hollow sound that sent a shiver down my spine. The kind of laugh that told me he enjoyed this— enjoyed seeing me cower beneath him, broken and afraid. "You think you have a choice?" he scoffed, his words hanging in the air like a death sentence. "You were supposed to be mine, Mia. You fucking gave yourself to Romeo, didn't you?" His eyes flashed with anger at the mention of the name, his voice dripping with hatred. "That boils my blood, you know that?"

The shift in his demeanor was unnerving. One moment, he was furious, consumed by rage, and the next, he was eerily calm, his expression softening as he took a step closer to me. "But you'll come around, won't you, Mia?" His voice was dangerously sweet now, like poisoned honey. "Because I love you. I always have." He crouched down in front of me, his hand reaching out to tilt my chin up, forcing me to meet his eyes. "Do you love me?" he asked, his tone almost tender. "Promise me you'll be my obedient girl again."

I could feel my stomach churn at his words, bile rising in my throat as I struggled to keep the disgust from showing on my face. "I can't love someone who treats me like this,"

I managed to say, though my voice wavered with the weight of fear pressing down on me.

Jamie's smile faded, replaced by pure amusement. "You think you have a choice, don't you?" His grip tightened on my chin, forcing my head back painfully. "Such a naïve little girl," he muttered, his lips brushing dangerously close to mine before he finally released me, standing up and walking toward the door. "But you'll learn. You'll fucking learn."

He left the room, and for a moment, I was alone, the silence pressing in around me like a suffocating blanket. My chest heaved, my breath ragged as I tried to process the pain coursing through my body, the overwhelming sense of helplessness threatening to drown me. But the respite was short-lived.

When Jamie returned, he carried a tray of food—if it could even be called that. A piece of stale bread and a bowl of watery soup. The sight of it only added to the knot of dread in my stomach. He set the tray down with an exaggerated flourish, the cigarette still burning between his lips as smoke curled lazily around his head. "Eat up, Mia," he purred, his voice dripping with false kindness. "You'll need your strength."

I stared at the tray, my stomach churning with nausea, but I forced myself to pick up the spoon. The taste was bland, the food unappetizing, but I ate, chewing slowly, my body trembling with exhaustion and fear. Jamie watched me the entire time, his eyes never leaving my face, as though he derived some sick pleasure from the sight of me eating, broken and defeated.

"You're not going to starve, Mia. I won't let that happen," he said after a while, leaning in close enough that I could smell the acrid scent of smoke on his breath. "You belong to me. I'll take care of you."

After I finished, Jamie ordered me to shower. I obeyed, my body moving on autopilot as I stumbled through the motions, the hot water scalding my skin but doing nothing to wash away the pain or the terror that clung to me like a second skin. Even as I stood there, naked and vulnerable, I could feel his presence just beyond the door, a constant reminder that I was never truly alone.

When I emerged, I found my clothes had been changed— neatly folded on the bed, clean but unfamiliar. Jamie stood in the corner, cigarette in hand, his red eyes gleaming in the dim light. "Look at you," he mused, his voice low and dangerous. "So beautiful, my marked girl."

He stepped toward me, slow and deliberate, his gaze dark and possessive. Before I could react, he pressed the burning tip of his cigarette against my skin, the searing pain shooting through me like fire. I gasped, biting back a scream as the skin blistered beneath the heat, his mark now burned into me, permanent and unyielding.

"See that?" Jamie murmured, tracing the raw wound with his fingers, his voice soft and almost tender. "You're mine now, Mia. No one else will ever touch you the way I do."

Tears welled up in my eyes as he leaned down, his lips capturing mine in a brutal kiss, his teeth sinking into my lower lip hard enough to draw blood. I tasted the bitter tang of iron mixed with the acrid smoke of his breath, the pain overwhelming, suffocating.

"Fucking bitch," he growled as he pulled away, his voice thick with rage. "You taste like Romeo."

Without warning, he slapped me hard across the face, the impact sending me sprawling to the floor. My vision blurred with the force of it, my cheek burning with the sting of his hand. "You're a monster," I choked out, my voice trembling with both fear and fury. "You're sick."

Jamie's face contorted with rage, his eyes blazing with an intensity that sent another wave of fear crashing over me. "You think I care what you think?" he spat, his voice low and dangerous. "You think any of this matters?"

Then, without warning, he kicked me hard in the ribs, the force of the blow knocking the wind from my lungs. I doubled over, gasping for air, coughing up blood and bile as pain wracked my body.

But even as I lay there, broken and gasping for breath, I heard it—the sound of footsteps approaching. My heart surged with hope, a tiny spark in the darkness that consumed me. Could it be? Was he really here?

The door swung open, and there he was—Romeo, his face etched with horror and rage as he took in the scene before him. His eyes locked on mine, widening with shock as he saw the state I was in.

"Let her go!" Romeo's voice thundered through the room, filled with fury and righteous anger, the sound of it cutting through the suffocating silence like a knife.

Jamie turned to face him, a cruel smile twisting his lips. "Ah, Romeo," he drawled, his voice dripping with mockery. "Come to save your precious Mia, have you? How noble."

The tension in the room was palpable, the air thick with the weight of everything that was about to unfold. My pulse raced, my heart pounding in my chest as I watched the two men face off, knowing that this moment would change everything.

CHAPTER THIRTY- SEVEN

ROMEO GIUSEPPE

Emerging from the derelict hospital, my heart sank deeper with every step I took. The grim reality that I couldn't find Mia weighed on me like a lead blanket, suffocating every thought. "Where could she be?" I muttered under my breath, frustration clawing at my insides. I was too late.

The eerie quiet of the hospital grounds lingered, an oppressive silence that only intensified the crushing guilt inside me. The building behind me, once filled with echoes of life, now stood as a hollow reminder of all the places I had searched in vain. Its faded, crumbling walls seemed to mock me, like the pieces of a puzzle I couldn't solve. My throat tightened as I realized how close I had been—and yet, how far.

Running my hands through my hair, I struggled to make sense of it all. Jamie had outsmarted me. No, not Jamie. He had been right under my nose this entire time, masquerading as someone he wasn't, and I had fallen for it—hard. The weight of my stupidity crashed over me, each realization hitting like a punch to the gut.

As I drove through the city, the blur of lights outside the window felt distant, insignificant. The rain splattered against the windshield, each drop an echo of the torment churning in my chest. I gripped the steering wheel tighter, my knuckles blanching, the world outside nothing but a storm of color and shadow. All I could think about was Mia—her laughter, her warmth—now replaced by an unbearable silence. Each mile felt like another step away from her, the pit in my stomach growing deeper.

I couldn't shake the last memory I had of her, the way her eyes sparkled when she laughed, the light in her smile. That light was extinguished now, taken from me, from us. She was lost somewhere in the dark, and I couldn't reach her. The thought made my heart race, thundering in my chest like a war drum.

Even the hackers I'd hired—some of the best in the business—couldn't trace her. Leo had covered his tracks too well. That bastard was always one step ahead, and now

Mia was suffering because of it. My failure weighed on me like a noose tightening around my neck, slowly suffocating me with each passing second. Every lead I followed, every road I drove down—nothing. It was as if she had vanished into thin air, leaving behind only a void where she used to be.

By the time I pulled into my driveway, one thought consumed me: I couldn't do this alone. The mansion stood cold and imposing before me, its grand façade doing nothing to comfort the emptiness gnawing at my soul. I stepped out into the rain, letting the cold water drench my skin as I made my way inside. My heart felt like it was tearing apart, the helplessness seeping deeper with every heartbeat.

I grabbed my phone, my fingers trembling as I dialed Eliseo's number. He was a man of influence, with connections to the CIA, FBI, and a reputation for digging up the truth no matter how well hidden it was.

The phone rang three times before he answered, his voice smooth but cautious. "Romeo?"

"Eliseo," I said, my voice tense, mixing English and Italian out of sheer habit. "Mia's been taken by Leo—Jamie, whatever the hell he calls himself. It's... a long story. I need your help. Can you come over tomorrow morning?"

There was a pause, the line quiet, and for a moment I thought he might refuse. But then, his voice returned, calm and steady. "I'll be there, Romeo," he replied, his voice laden with sympathy. "Your family... what they did for mine—I'm indebted for life. We'll get her back."

"Grazie," I said, exhaling a breath I hadn't realized I was holding. "I won't forget this."

Hanging up the phone, I stood in the middle of the room, the weight of everything crashing down on me. The night stretched out before me, an endless, suffocating abyss. I barely slept, my mind replaying the moments over and over—every sign I missed, every opportunity I had to stop this before it spiraled out of control. Leo had been with me from the start, orchestrating everything. The thought gnawed at me, turning guilt into rage.

How had I not seen it? Leo—the man I trusted with my life, my right-hand man—had betrayed me. The realization felt like a knife twisting in my gut. I had let him get close, let him manipulate everything, and now Mia was paying the price for my blindness. Sleep was impossible, my mind trapped in an endless loop of regret and anger. Each second felt like a blade slicing through me, the guilt consuming everything.

When Eliseo arrived, the air was thick with tension. The sun had barely risen, casting an ominous light over the mansion, but we didn't have time to waste. Eliseo was all business, his face set in grim determination as he moved quickly to set up his equipment in my living room. Screens flickered with data and code—details that meant nothing to me but everything to him. He worked with the precision of a surgeon, his eyes never leaving the display.

I paced the floor, feeling the walls of my home close in around me. Each second that passed felt like an eternity, each breath heavier than the last. Anxiety gnawed at me. Mia was out there, trapped, and all I could do was wait. My fists clenched, knuckles turning white. The silence stretched on, every passing second feeling like a nail in my coffin.

Finally, Eliseo turned, his face pale with revelation. "Romeo, Leo—your bodyguard—he's been playing you the entire time."

The weight of his words hit me like a freight train. I staggered back, my mind reeling. "How... how could I have been so blind?"

Eliseo typed furiously, pulling up more information. "He planned it perfectly, covering his tracks. Leo even made sure you thought he was dead."

A tidal wave of disbelief crashed over me. The one person I trusted with my life had been behind it all. Rage boiled in my veins, but beneath it, the sting of betrayal cut deeper than anything I had ever felt. The memories of every conversation, every shared moment with Leo, twisted into something dark, sinister.

"Marcus was with you the day Mia was taken, right?" Eliseo continued, eyes glued to the screen. "Leo must have made his move then. He's a mastermind, Romeo. He's been controlling this from the start."

I shook my head, my breath hitching. "Dio mio, I should have trusted my instincts. I should have known."

Eliseo didn't stop, his fingers moving across the keyboard like a surgeon. "We'll find them. I'm narrowing down the possible locations now."

I barely heard him over the roar of fury inside me. Leo— that bastard, that traitor—had twisted everything. He took Mia, and he was going to pay for it.

"We've got something," Eliseo said, his voice pulling me back to reality. He pointed to the screen. "There's movement near an abandoned hospital on the outskirts of the city. It fits Leo's pattern—isolated, easy to defend."

My chest tightened. "That's where she is."

Eliseo turned to face me, his expression grim. "Romeo, listen. Leo will be expecting you. He knows you'll come for her. This won't be easy."

I met his gaze, cold determination hardening inside me. "I don't care how dangerous it is. I'm going to get her back."

"We'll go in prepared," Eliseo said, standing up. "But you need to be smart about this. Leo is dangerous. He won't hesitate."

I nodded, though inside, all I felt was the fire of vengeance. "Thank you, Eliseo. I'll make sure this is worth your while."

He shook his head. "You don't owe me anything, Romeo."

But I did. I owed Mia her safety, her freedom—everything that had been ripped away by the monster who was once my friend.

As the day of the invasion approached, I gathered my men. We prepared, planning every detail down to the last second. Eliseo was right—Leo would expect us. But I wouldn't let him win.

CHAPTER THIRTY- EIGHT

ROMEO GIUSEPPE

As I stood frozen in the doorway, the harrowing sight before me ignited a firestorm of emotions—rage, fear, and desperation swirling together into an unstoppable force that coiled tightly in my chest. The room, once a cold, sterile chamber in an abandoned hospital, now felt like a battlefield. Mia lay crumpled on the dirty floor, bruised and battered, her once fierce spirit barely a flicker in her eyes.

The light that used to dance there had been dimmed, replaced with the haunted look of someone pushed to their very limits. I felt the ground shift beneath me as I struggled to contain the fury boiling just below the surface.

Jamie, that twisted bastard, stood over her, his sickening grin stretched across his face, reveling in the torment he had caused. His eyes gleamed with the triumph of a man who thought he had won—a man who believed he had broken her. But I wasn't going to let him walk away from this.

"Let her go!" The words tore from my throat, ripping through the cold, damp air with a force that startled even me. My voice, normally calm and measured, boomed like thunder, shaking the walls of this forsaken place. The intensity of my command reverberated in my ears, but Jamie's smirk only deepened, his eyes flicking lazily toward me as if I were nothing more than an afterthought in his game.

"Ah, Romeo," Jamie sneered, his voice dripping with condescension and cruelty. He straightened himself, standing taller, more confident. "So you've come to save your precious Mia." His gaze traveled to her broken form, and I saw the twisted pleasure he took in seeing her like this. "How noble of you. But don't you see? It's too late. She's already mine."

Every word that dripped from his lips ignited a new wave of fury inside me. My fists clenched at my sides, and I could feel my heart hammering wildly against my ribs.

Jamie wasn't just a man standing before me—he was a monster. A monster who had manipulated and twisted everything good in Mia's life, a betrayal deeper than any wound I had ever suffered.

"Stay the hell away from her, Jamie," I growled, each word laced with venom. I stepped further into the room, my movements deliberate and measured, though inside, I was barely holding onto control. The air between us was heavy with unspoken threats, a tension so thick it suffocated the very space we stood in.

Jamie chuckled darkly, his eyes gleaming with malicious amusement. "You think you can just walk in here and take her? She belongs to me now, Romeo. Look at her." He waved a hand toward Mia, her fragile body trembling as she tried to pull herself together. "She's mine. She knows it, and you know it. You've already lost."

The heat surged in my chest, burning hotter than I could ever remember. My vision tunneled, and all I could see was Jamie—the source of all this pain and misery. "You've twisted her mind, manipulated her, but that's over now.

I'm not letting you destroy her any more than you already have."

For a split second, I saw a flicker of fear in Mia's eyes, her lips parting as she struggled to speak. "Romeo... I—" But before she could finish, Jamie's hand moved with lightning speed, slapping her hard across the face. The sharp crack echoed through the room, sending shockwaves straight into my core. Her head snapped to the side, and she collapsed in a heap, a soft, broken sob escaping her lips.

That was the moment my control shattered.

"Non più!" The roar that erupted from me came from a place so deep inside, I barely recognized it as my voice. Without thinking, I reached beneath my jacket, my fingers curling around the cold, unforgiving steel of my pistol. The weight of the gun in my hand brought a strange sense of clarity, like the final piece of a puzzle snapping into place. I raised it, aiming directly at Jamie's chest, the target so clear, so undeniable.

"Let her go," I growled, my voice low and deadly, "or I swear to God, I will end you right here."

Jamie's smile never faltered. If anything, it grew wider. "Do you really think you can kill me, Romeo?" he asked, almost laughing at the absurdity of my threat. "You have no idea who you're dealing with. You've always been the one playing catch-up, haven't you?"

He took a step closer to Mia, his boots crunching against the debris on the floor. Then, without warning, he stepped on her stomach, grinding his heel down with sadistic glee. A pained gasp escaped her, and I could see her body trembling in agony.

"Are you ready to be my obedient girl again?" Jamie taunted, his voice dripping with venom as he leaned in closer to her. His fingers traced the bruises along her jawline before he bent down and forcefully kissed her, a grotesque display of dominance that turned my stomach.

"Get away from her!" My voice was raw with rage, my hands trembling as I tightened my grip on the gun. My pulse raced in my ears, and every part of me screamed for violence, for retribution. I leveled the gun at Jamie, my finger poised on the trigger.

He sneered, his lips curling as he pulled back. "She tastes like you, Romeo," he said, his voice dripping with malice. "That's what makes it all the more enjoyable."

The moment those words left his mouth, I didn't hesitate. I squeezed the trigger, and the gunshot rang out like thunder in the enclosed room. The bullet tore through the air, striking Jamie square in the chest with brutal precision. His smirk faltered, and his eyes widened in shock as he stumbled backward, clutching his chest where the blood was now seeping through his fingers.

Time seemed to slow as he fell to the floor, his body hitting the ground with a heavy thud. His eyes, once full of cruel amusement, were now filled with disbelief as the life drained from him.

"Mia!" I was at her side in an instant, dropping to my knees on the cold, hard floor. My hands gently cupped her face, the warmth of her skin beneath my palms a relief, though her body trembled in my arms. "I've got you," I whispered, pulling her into me, feeling the fragile strength in her as she clung to me like I was her lifeline. "We're leaving this place. I'm not letting him hurt you anymore."

Her tears spilled down her cheeks, a mixture of pain, relief, and terror in her eyes as she clutched onto me. "I... I was so scared, Romeo," she sobbed, her voice barely above a whisper. "I didn't think you'd come for me."

"Shh," I murmured, holding her tightly against my chest, cradling her as if she might shatter if I let go. "It's over. I'm here now. You're safe. I swear, I won't let anyone hurt you ever again."

The weight of what I had just done, what we had both endured, pressed down on me, but I pushed it away. This wasn't the time for reflection. Mia was what mattered now—her safety, her recovery. Everything else could wait.

As I lifted her into my arms, her body weak but alive, I could feel her fingers gripping my shirt, her sobs muffled against my chest. I carried her out of the darkness, away from the hell Jamie had created. The cold night air hit my skin as we stepped outside, but it felt like freedom.

The nightmare was over.

And with Mia in my arms, we would face whatever came next together.

CHAPTER THIRTY- NINE

ROMEO GIUSEPPE

I held Mia close, her trembling body a testament to the nightmares that still haunted her. "Hey, I'm here," I whispered, my lips brushing against her silken hair, the familiar scent of jasmine and vanilla soothing my frayed nerves. "Sono qui, amore mio," I added, using the Italian endearment that always seemed to calm her restless spirit.

The warmth of her body against mine grounded me, anchoring me in this moment.
Her eyes fluttered open, revealing the fear lingering in their depths like shadows that refused to fade. "The nightmares... they're getting worse," she confessed, her voice barely above a whisper, a haunting echo of her pain.

My heart ached, knowing that the memories of being held captive by Leo—or Jamie, as I now knew him—still clung to her like a shroud, a constant reminder of her trauma.

Anger surged toward my brother, but I pushed it aside, focusing solely on Mia's needs as she fought through the darkness threatening to engulf her.

After the incident, Mia had undergone surgery to repair her physical injuries, but the emotional scars ran deeper than any incision. Each day, I witnessed her struggle, the shadows of her past creeping into our present. I had been by her side every step of the way, determined to be her unwavering support.

That's why I encouraged her to see Alessia Mattia, a therapist specializing in trauma. I accompanied Mia to her sessions, holding her hand through the tough moments, offering silent support as she faced her demons head-on.

Today's session was particularly difficult. Alessia guided Mia through the labyrinth of her thoughts, her voice a steady beacon in the turbulent sea of emotions. I could see the pain etched on Mia's face, a tapestry of suffering woven with threads of resilience.

"Mia, can you tell me about the nightmares?" Alessia asked gently, her tone as soft as a whispering breeze, coaxing Mia to share her burdens.

Mia's voice trembled as she spoke. "I see Jamie's face... I feel trapped and helpless, like I'm suffocating in a cage of my own making," she replied, her words laced with desperation, each syllable a fragile thread pulling at my heart.

I squeezed her hand, trying to convey my unwavering love and support, feeling the warmth of her skin against mine— a reminder that she was still here, still fighting.
Alessia nodded, her expression a mixture of empathy and determination. "We'll work through this, Mia. You're not alone. You have the strength within you to break free from these chains," she assured, her words wrapping around Mia like a comforting blanket.

As we left the session, the air felt heavy with the weight of Mia's struggles, yet I was resolved to be her anchor. The sunlight filtered through the trees, casting dappled patterns on the ground, but the warmth of the day did little to dispel the chill in the air.

Later that afternoon, I took Mia to the park, where we sat on a weathered bench overlooking the shimmering lake. The sun dipped low on the horizon, painting the sky with hues of gold and pink. I took her hand in mine, tracing the scars on her wrist—each mark a testament to her survival, a reminder of battles fought and won.

"Queste cicatrici non ti definiscono, Mia. Sono un promemoria di ciò che hai superato," I said softly, my voice a soothing balm. Those scars didn't define her; they were reminders of her strength, of battles fought and won.

Mia's eyes welled up with tears, but this time, they were tears of hope—glimmers of light breaking through the darkness. She leaned into me, her head resting on my shoulder, and for a moment, everything felt right in the world.

"Grazie, Romeo," she whispered, her voice laced with gratitude. "I don't know what I'd do without you."

I held her close, feeling my heart swell with love and pride. "Non dovrai mai scoprirlo, Mia. Sarò sempre qui per te," I replied, assuring her she'd never have to find out because I'd always be there for her, a steadfast presence in her life. As the sun dipped below the horizon, painting the sky with a fiery glow, I knew that Mia was going to be okay. She was healing, and I felt honored to be by her side every step of the way.

In other news, my parents, Mr. and Mrs. Aurelio Giuseppe, had taken notice of Mia's unwavering dedication to her perfume business, Mia Floré. They saw an opportunity to combine their philanthropic efforts with Mia's expertise and creativity.

Mrs. Giuseppe approached Mia with an idea that sparkled with potential: to create a bespoke fragrance for the Giuseppe Foundation's annual charity gala. The fragrance would be auctioned off, with proceeds going toward the foundation's scholarship program—an initiative that could change lives.
Mia's face lit up with enthusiasm, her eyes shining like stars. "I would love to!" she exclaimed, her passion

infectious. She poured her heart into creating a stunning fragrance, "Eleganza," featuring notes of bergamot, rose, and sandalwood. The scent was elegant and sophisticated, a true reflection of her spirit, and it would be perfect for the charity gala.

As the event approached, Mia and I worked tirelessly together to promote the fragrance and the foundation's noble mission. We spent long evenings brainstorming ideas, crafting promotional materials, and meeting with potential donors. Our combined efforts resulted in a highly successful gala, with "Eleganza" fetching a record price at the auction. My parents were overjoyed with the outcome, and Mia's business received invaluable exposure. I beamed with pride, witnessing my loved ones making a positive impact together, each moment a testament to our strength.

In the aftermath of the gala, we received countless compliments, and Mia's confidence soared. She glowed with a sense of accomplishment, her spirit rekindled like a flame emerging from the ashes.

"Mia, you did an incredible job," I said as we walked home, the night air filled with the sounds of celebration fading into the distance. "You've proven that you're more than what happened to you. You're a force to be reckoned with."

Her smile was radiant, the light returning to her eyes. "I couldn't have done it without your support, Romeo. You believed in me when I didn't believe in myself," she replied, her voice thick with emotion, a mix of gratitude and determination.

I squeezed her hand, feeling a rush of affection. "Always. I'll be your biggest supporter, no matter what."

As we reached my apartment, I paused and turned to her, a thought striking me like a bolt of lightning. "What if we take this further? What if we expand Mia Floré? This could be just the beginning for you."

Mia's eyes widened, and I could see the wheels turning in her mind, the spark of possibility igniting her imagination. "You mean, like a whole line of fragrances?" she asked, her excitement palpable.

"Exactly. We could work on a series inspired by different themes, emotions, and memories—each fragrance telling a story.

You have a talent for this, and I want the world to see it," I said, my heart racing with the vision of our future coming together, each step bringing us closer to realizing her dreams.

Her face lit up with excitement, a beautiful glow radiating from within. "That sounds amazing, Romeo! I've always dreamed of creating something beautiful and meaningful," she exclaimed, her eyes shining with possibility.

I smiled, the vision of our future solidifying like the first rays of dawn breaking through the night. "And we'll do it together. I'll handle the business side, and you can focus on the creative aspects. It's time to turn your dreams into reality."

Mia threw her arms around me, and I held her tightly, feeling the warmth of her spirit reigniting my own. "Thank you for believing in me. I don't think I could face the future without you."

As we stood there, wrapped in each other's embrace, I knew that the journey ahead would have its challenges, but together, we would navigate through them. Our love was stronger than the darkness we had faced, and as long as we had each other, we could conquer anything.

With her by my side, I felt ready to take on the world, knowing that together we could build a future that would shine brighter than the stars above, illuminating the path we were destined to walk.

EPILOGUE

MIA BIANCHI

I, Mia Giuseppe, stood on the stage, the bright lights casting a warm glow on my face as I gazed out at the sea of faces before me. The launch of "Rinascita," a program dedicated to empowering women who have experienced domestic violence, felt like a surreal dream come true. Beside me stood my loving husband, Romeo, his eyes shimmering with pride, reflecting the warmth of his unwavering support and love.

"Rinascita" aimed to create a sanctuary where women could share their stories, find solace, and embark on their journeys to healing. The energy in the room was palpable, each woman carrying her unique tale of struggle and resilience. As I looked out at the audience, I could see their nervous smiles and hopeful expressions, a beautiful tapestry of emotions woven together by shared experiences.

Taking a deep breath, I inhaled the mingling scents of fresh flowers and anticipation, my heart pounding with excitement and anxiety. I felt the gentle squeeze of Romeo's hand, his touch igniting a sense of calm within me, grounding me in this moment.

"Welcome, everyone, to Rinascita," I began, my voice steady yet filled with emotion. "This program is for you and because of you. Your stories, your strength, and your courage inspired me to create this haven."

The room erupted in applause, a thunderous wave of encouragement that washed over me, fueling my purpose. The applause felt like a heartbeat, resonating with the hope and determination that filled the space. I glanced at the women in the audience, their eyes shimmering with tears of joy and gratitude, and I felt a rush of connection, a bond that transcended words.

"Grazie mille," I said, my voice thick with gratitude as I thanked them in Italian. "Your support means the world to me."

After the session, women approached me, their eyes glistening with unshed tears, sharing their personal stories. I watched as Romeo listened intently, offering words of encouragement and support, his presence a lighthouse guiding them through their storms. One woman, Sarah, stepped forward, her hands trembling slightly as she grasped my hand tightly.

"Thank you, Mia. I thought I was alone. But hearing your story and the others... I feel seen. I feel heard," she whispered, her voice barely above a whisper, but her sincerity pierced through the noise of the crowd.

When I met Romeo's gaze, I saw the understanding and love reflected in me, a silent promise that we were in this together. He squeezed my hand gently, his warmth wrapping around me like a protective cocoon.

"Ti amo," I whispered, letting him know just how profoundly he meant to me, my heart swelling with affection, a silent declaration of gratitude for his unwavering support.

As the weeks rolled by, "Rinascita" flourished, transforming into a vibrant community of connection and support. Women found solace in each other's company, their laughter mingling with tears of joy as they formed bonds that transcended their pasts. Each session felt like a celebration of strength and resilience, and Romeo attended every single one, his steadfast presence a constant reminder of the power of love and support.

One evening, as we nestled together on our couch, the soft glow of the lamp casting a warm halo around us, Romeo turned to me, his expression serious yet full of admiration.

"Mia, I'm so proud of you," he said, his voice rich with sincerity. "You're changing lives, amore mio."

I smiled, feeling my heart swell with joy, warmth radiating through me. "We're changing lives, Romeo. Together," I replied, the warmth of unity filling the air, a shared heartbeat echoing between us.

"Insieme," I added, emphasizing our bond in Italian, each syllable a reaffirmation of our shared journey and commitment to one another.

As I gazed into his eyes, a wave of contentment washed over me. Our journey had been marked by trials and tribulations, but in that moment, everything felt perfectly aligned, as if the universe conspired to bring us to this point of harmony.

Just then, our triplets, Enzo, Matteo, and Giulia, burst into the room, their laughter and energy infectious, flooding the space with joy. Enzo, our little adventurer, was always getting into mischief; his curious nature and fearless spirit inspired us daily. Matteo, our gentle soul, radiated kindness, reminding me of the beauty of compassion with his empathetic heart. And then there was Giulia, our little diva—a force to be reckoned with; her confidence and creativity brightened our lives in a way that only she could, her laughter a melody that danced through the air.

"Mommy, Mommy! We made a picture for you!" Giulia exclaimed, thrusting a colorful drawing into my hands, her eyes sparkling with pride, the artwork a whirlwind of colors that reflected her vibrant spirit.

My heart swelled as I looked at it, the vibrant colors a testament to her imagination. "It's beautiful, amore mia! I love it so much!" I declared, my voice laced with genuine affection, my heart swelling with pride for my little artist.

Romeo chuckled, scooping up Enzo and Matteo in a big hug, their laughter ringing through our home like music, a symphony of joy that resonated in my heart. "And what about us, boys? Don't we get pictures too?" he teased, his playful tone inviting giggles from our children.

Laughter erupted in the room, and I felt a joy I never thought possible. We were a family, a unit forged through love and resilience, and nothing could ever break that bond. The walls of our home echoed with love, and I reveled in the blissful chaos that filled our lives.

Having survived domestic violence, I had reclaimed my identity, rewriting my story in vibrant strokes of hope and healing. My little boys were overly protective of their sister, often teasing her and their father by affectionately calling them "Little Romeos." The playful banter filled our home with laughter, and I cherished every moment, knowing how far we had come.

As we settled back onto the couch, I reflected on the incredible journey that lay behind us. The path to recovery hadn't been easy, but with every step, I felt stronger and more resilient. I hoped my story would inspire others, just as their stories had profoundly impacted me, lighting the way for those still navigating the shadows.

"Hey, kids," I said, my voice brightening with excitement, a glimmer of mischief dancing in my eyes. "How about we celebrate our first successful session with some ice cream?"

"Yay!" they cheered in unison, their eyes lighting up with pure joy and excitement, the sound a sweet melody that resonated in my heart.

As we prepared for our impromptu ice cream party, I caught Romeo's gaze, feeling a surge of gratitude. "Thank you for being my rock, Romeo. I couldn't have done this without you," I said, my heart full, the words heavy with meaning.

He smiled, leaning closer, his voice low and sincere. "And I'll always be here for you, Mia. No matter what," he promised, his words a soothing balm that wrapped around my soul, fortifying our bond and igniting the fire of our love.

With that promise lingering in the air, I knew our journey with Rinascita was just the beginning. Together, we would create a legacy of hope, love, and strength for all the women who walked through our doors. Each shared story would be a thread in a larger tapestry of resilience, weaving connections and uplifting spirits.

As the laughter of our children filled the room, I felt the weight of the world lift from my shoulders, replaced by an overwhelming sense of purpose. This was more than just a program; it was a movement, a revolution of empowerment that would echo through generations. With each woman who found their voice and each story that emerged, we would continue to heal, uplift, and inspire, planting seeds of hope that would blossom in the hearts of those we touched.

RESOURCES AND SUPPORT

If you or someone you know is experiencing domestic violence, abuse, or manipulation, please reach out to:

- National Domestic Violence Hotline (1-800-799-7233).
- National Sexual Assault Hotline (1-800-656-HOPE).
- National Dating Abuse Helpline (1-866-331-9474)

SIGNS OF ABUSE:

- Physical: bruises, injuries, or control over daily activities.
- Emotional: constant criticism, belittling, or isolation.
- Verbal: name-calling, threats, or constant monitoring.
- Financial: control over finances or resources.

WHEN TO SEEK HELP:

- If you feel scared, trapped, or controlled.

- If you're experiencing physical or emotional harm.
- If you're being isolated from friends and family.
- If you're being forced into sexual activities

REMEMBER:

- You are not alone.
- You deserve respect and love.
- There is help available.

ACKNOWLEDEMENTS

I want to extend my deepest gratitude to those who have supported me through the twisted and tumultuous journey of writing this book. To my loved ones, thank you for your unwavering encouragement and patience, even when the darkness of these characters' worlds seeped into my own. To my editor, your keen eye and insightful guidance helped shape this story into the haunting tale it is today.

And to my readers, I'm eternally grateful for your bravery in embracing the shadows alongside me. Your enthusiasm and loyalty mean everything.

This book was shaped in silence, rewritten in exhaustion, and finished with nothing but stubborn love. I edited and proofread it myself, line by line, breath by breath. Because I believed in the story enough to carry it alone. The cover art design was designed by me, using Canva.

AUTHOR'S NOTE

This story was born from shadows, where love dances with obsession, and loyalty is a double-edged sword.
Dangerous Obsession is not a tale of gentle romance. It is raw, dark, and often uncomfortable. These characters live in a world ruled by crime, trauma, and unforgiving choices. Their love is destructive, complicated, and deeply human.

I wrote this for readers who crave the beauty within the broken, who understand that healing doesn't always come wrapped in kindness. There is no perfection here, only flawed souls navigating the chaos of loyalty, power, and impossible love.

Please take care while reading. The content explores heavy emotional themes, and I encourage checking the trigger warnings listed.

Thank you for stepping into this world with me.
Blue Winter

SNEAK PEEK PREVIEW

Dangerous Obsession

"Power breeds loyalty. But obsession? Obsession destroys everything."

Evra Giuseppe was raised in a world where bloodlines mean everything, and trust means nothing. When a calculated attack by a rival mafia family shatters her reality, she's thrust into a violent web of ancient feuds and dangerous allegiances.

Enter Alessandro Dante—ruthless, cold, and hell-bent on revenge. His obsession with power is matched only by his desire to possess Evra, no matter the cost. But when hatred turns into something far more twisted, Evra must decide: Is love just another weapon in the wrong hands?

With betrayal around every corner and desire that cuts deeper than any blade, Evra's path to survival means confronting her past, redefining loyalty, and discovering just how far she'll go to reclaim her power.

Get ready for a dark, seductive journey through the mafia underworld.

Dangerous Obsession: Book One of *Devious Series*
Coming out on October 31st, 2024

Genre: Dark Romance, Mafia Fiction, Psychological Thriller

BOOKS WRITTEN BY BLUE WINTER

Dark Beauty

In the mystical realm of Tenebrous, where ancient magic reigns, Giovanni Fabiano, a powerful vampire mafia boss, has been cursed by a vengeful witch to walk alone for eternity. For centuries, he has searched for a way to break the curse, but to no avail.

Sophia Greene, a beautiful and fiercely independent young woman, unknowingly holds the key to Giovanni's salvation. When their paths cross, a forbidden love ignites, threatening to destroy the very fabric of their worlds. As they navigate treacherous landscapes and battle dark forces, Giovanni and Sophia must confront the curse and their own destinies. Will their love be strong enough to overcome the darkness, or will the witch's curse forever condemn them to solitude?

BUY NOW ON AMAZON

Dangerous Obsession

In a world where loyalty is paramount, a forbidden love sparks a deadly war. Romeo Giuseppe, a ruthless mafia enforcer, is bound by duty and loyalty to his family.

But everything changes when he falls for Mia Bianchi, his sister's best friend. Their love, once a source of joy, quickly transforms into a dangerous liability, threatening to upend the fragile peace between their two families.

As their relationship deepens, loyalties are tested, and hidden truths unravel. Romeo finds himself torn between his heart and his duty, navigating the treacherous underworld of mafia politics, where one misstep can be fatal. Meanwhile, Mia's ex-fiancée, Jamie, is determined to destroy their love and claim power for himself.

With both families vying for control and secrets threatening to tear them apart, Romeo and Mia's love becomes a beacon of hope in a world consumed by darkness. But can their love survive the danger that surrounds them?

As the stakes rise, Romeo must confront the reality that the loyalty and duty that once bound him may become the very forces that threaten their happiness. In this gripping tale of love, loyalty, and power, the consequences are deadly, and the question remains: will their love endure or succumb to the chaos of the world they inhabit?

Genre: Dark Romance, Crime, Psychological Thiller

BUY NOW ON AMAZON

BOOKS IN THE SERIES

Devious Series

Welcome to the Devious series, where passion and obsession collide with secrets and lies. In this twisted world of rival families, hidden agendas, and forbidden desires, nothing is as it seems.

Follow the complex characters as they navigate love, loyalty, and betrayal, all while facing the darkness within themselves. Each book in the series will keep you on the edge of your seat, wondering what's real and what's just a deception.

Dangerous Obsession

In a world where loyalty is everything, forbidden love ignites a deadly war. Romeo Giuseppe, a ruthless mafia enforcer, is bound by duty to his family—until he falls for Mia Bianchi, his sister's best friend.

Their secret love threatens to unravel the fragile peace between rival families, as loyalty is tested and dangerous secrets come to light.

Caught in a treacherous "web of mafia politics, Romeo must choose between his heart and his duty.

But Mia's vengeful ex-fiancée, Jamie, will stop at nothing to destroy them and seize power. As rival families vie for control, Romeo and Mia's love becomes a beacon of hope in a world of darkness.

Can their love survive the looming danger, or will the very loyalty that binds Romeo be the thing that destroys their chance at happiness?

Genre: Dark Romance, Crime, Psychological Thiller

BUY NOW ON AMAZON

CONTACT INFORMATION

For updates and more information about upcoming books, visit my Goodreads Page: Blue Winter.

Follow Blue Winter on:
Instagram:@bluewinterwrites
TikTok: @bluewinterauthor_
Facebook: @blue winter
Pinterest: @bluewinter_auth

www.ingramcontent.com/pod-product-compliance
Lightning Source LLC
Chambersburg PA
CBHW020415030726
47495CB00006B/1510